Think
Fast,
Mr. Peters

Think
Fast,
Mr. Peters

Stuart Kaminsky

St. Martin's Press • New York

Library of Congress Cataloging-in-Publication Data

Kaminsky, Stuart M.
 Think fast, Mr. Peters / by Stuart Kaminsky.
  p. cm.
 "A Thomas Dunne Book"
 ISBN 0-312-01520-8 : $15.95
 I. Title.
 PS3561.A43T5 1988
 813'.54—dc19   87-27616

First Edition

10 9 8 7 6 5 4 3 2 1

To Enid Lisa Perll with love

With thanks to Claude Chabrol
for the idea

Think
Fast,
Mr. Peters

1

Two German shepherds named Trudi and Heidi were about to claw their way through the cardboard door to the Victory Window of I. Magnin on Wilshire in the hope that they could tear me into Spam salad. The dogs were under the mistaken impression that I had, a few minutes earlier, shot a store guard named Murchison. If I hadn't dropped my gun in the menswear department, I'd have shot the dogs.

No one would have blamed me. No one trusted German shepherds. It was unpatriotic. People who owned them had started dropping the "German" and calling the dogs "shepherds," but those of us who had been around for more than half a decade weren't falling for it. Those Nazi dogs were the enemy. If we put Japanese Americans in prison camps for having Japanese ancestors, why weren't we interning dogs whose names were a challenge to the war effort?

My back was against the flimsy door, which shook with the assault by Trudi and Heidi. The dogs snarled, growled, and sank their teeth and claws into the door, which had been built for show and not for privacy or protection. I knew what the furry duo could do. They had already shredded the sleeve of my jacket and ripped the left knee of my pants. My knee was bleeding from a lunge by Heidi just as I had slammed the Window door. I reached out with one hand and kept my shoulders pressed against the door. My heels began to slip but my fingers touched a chair near the table in the window. Rudy Vallee had sat in the chair that very afternoon selling U.S.

War Savings Bonds and Stamps and autographing stamp albums and war bond applications. I had seen him grinning, adjusting his glasses, waving at the ladies on Wilshire. Now I shoved the wooden chair Vallee had been sitting in under the door handle as the Nazi canines went wild.

I looked around for other fortification. From the nearby wall, I plucked a neatly printed cardboard sign that informed me by the dim moonlight over Los Angeles that I would be complying with Federal Credit Regulation if payment for my charge purchases was made in full "on or before the tenth day of the second calendar month following the calendar month during which such article was sold." What the hell did that mean and what could I do with the sign, feed it to the canine krauts?

The tin screws on the door rattled as the hinges began to come loose. From the corner of my eye or the edge of my frenzy and imagination, I saw something move on Wilshire; someone was looking in the window. If the window had been lighted maybe a passing car, maybe even a cop, would have spotted me, but the war blackout had darkened Los Angeles after sundown. I looked down, sign in hand, into a pair of drunken eyes set deep in the skull of a broom-thin old man with a wild dirty-gray beard. He wore a coat and looked cold in spite of the summer heat. I gestured at the vibrating door behind me, mouthed "help," and considered a round of desperate charades. The old man grinned and showed a lone dark tooth in appreciation of my act.

The window was too thick to be heard through, and the man's stupor too dense to penetrate with my limited skills at mime. I searched for something to write a message with on the back of the sign. What the hell had Rudy Vallee signed all those stamp books with? Whatever it was, it wasn't in the goddamned Victory Window. I dropped the sign on the small table and dug madly in my pockets for something, anything to write with. I found some coins, the keys to my Crosley, a stick of Black Jack gum, and some lint.

A crack. The muzzle of one of the dogs ripped through the door. I turned to the old man and waved my arms. He did the same. I pointed at the door, at the snarling teeth of the dog. He did the same and grinned. I took a step toward him in frustration and my bleeding knee gave way. One-tooth stumbled in imitation and nearly had a stroke laughing. He tugged at his dirty beard and looked up and down the street for someone to share the show with. The son of a bitch was having a great time. I threw the sign at him and he jumped back when it hit the window. Suddenly, I wasn't fun anymore. He shoved his hands deep into his pockets, gave me a disapproving pout, and shuffled into the night.

It was slightly before midnight on Friday, June 12, 1942. I was almost fifty, missing my gun and one I'd borrowed from my landlady, out of suits, and almost out of time. Maybe this was it. I was going to die in the Victory Window of I. Magnin & Co. A small victory for the Axis. I didn't think the mangling of one weary private investigator would make up for the jolt the Nazis were taking at Sevastopol, but I—the door was about to go. I kicked the small table over. A wet throb of pain shot through my knee. I stumbled forward, grabbed the table, and shoved it against the chair, pushing with both hands, but it was clear that I was only buying a few seconds. There was no hoping for rescue by the night watchman Murchison. He was writhing around inside the store with a bullet in his leg.

I had a fee to collect, a hefty fraction of my life still to live, and an assortment of aches and bruises to take care of. There are some days it doesn't pay to get up off the floor.

"Shut up," I shouted at the determined dogs. I searched for some word in German. Maybe German shepherds understood German. Orders always sounded better in German, only I didn't know any German. I could offer them Black Jack gum, retrieve the cardboard sign as a useless weapon, or think of something clever. I let go of the chair and table, rolled to my feet, and threw myself against the window. I bounced off the glass and tripped backward. I didn't fall. I didn't cry. I turned, blew out a blast of air, and faced the door that now burst wide open, letting in the raging killer-dogs to claw their way over the chair and table.

Think fast, Toby Peters, I said, but no thought came.

It had all begun on Wednesday morning, at least the part that involved me. I'd been asleep on the floor of my room in Mrs. Plaut's boarding house on Heliotrope in Hollywood. I sleep on a mattress on the floor because of my bad back, one of the many parts of my body in need of disaster aid. The back had first acted up or reacted about seven years earlier when I had been a security guard at the premiere of a Mickey Rooney movie. A very large Negro gentleman had decided to welcome the Mick, and I made the mistake of getting in the way of the large man. Actually, it hadn't seemed like a mistake at the time. It was what I was getting paid twenty bucks for. The big man had lifted me in a bear hug and grunted till something in my lower back screeched like a two-timed woman. Since then my troubles and any changes in the weather tended to go for my back. A cold or a twist and turn the wrong way and I'm hobbling for a week and trying Egyptian remedies and faith healers.

My door had banged open that Wednesday morning followed by Mrs. Plaut, a small, ancient, gray stick of a creature in a black smock carrying a dust mop. Mrs. Plaut and the mop looked like twins. I had long given up asking or demanding that Mrs. Plaut knock at my door before entering. Pleas and threats were no use. They went through Mrs. Plaut's almost deaf ears without meeting resistance or acknowledgment. Physical barriers were equally useless. In spite of her seventy-plus years and her ninety-minus pounds, the woman was capable of rolling over the entire USC football team.

Mrs. Plaut had a hearing aid. I had given it to her, but it wasn't in her ear now.

"There is a telephone for you, Mr. Peelers," she announced much louder than the FBI when they surrounded Machine-Gun Kelly.

"I'm coming," I groaned, sitting up carefully. My back didn't protest but my arm felt more than a little numb. I'd just returned from a case in New York that netted me enough money to pay my room and office rent and buy me a week or two of tacos and a bottle of Shinola Dress Parade, which I planned to use with broad strokes on my only pair of shoes.

Mrs. Plaut stood, her vision perfect, scanning the mess in my room with disapproval. She wasn't leaving. I was wearing wrinkled boxer shorts and an undershirt just like the one Clark Gable had worn in *It Happened One Night*.

"The telephone is waiting," she said, pointing toward the open door with the dust mop.

"The telephone can wait," I said, getting up groggily. "My pants . . ."

"Put your pants on," she said, wielding her trusty mop like a pom-pom to indicate the general direction of my heaped trousers next to the ancient sofa.

I groped for the pants and glanced at the Beech-Nut gum clock on the wall near the door. It was a little after seven. I needed something wet in my mouth, coffee, and a bowl or two of Quaker Puffed Wheat or Rice with milk, but was afraid Mrs. Plaut would leap in front of me if I headed for the sink—fearful that she would raise her trusty mop and, like Tyrone Power in *Blood and Sand*, skewer me painfully in the gut.

The telephone was waiting.

I staggered across the room like a wounded bull, tried to get into my pants, and managed to succeed just short of the table in the alcove by the window. I considered asking Mrs. Plaut to simply take a message from the caller, but asking Mrs. Plaut to do such a thing would be far from simple. I had once spent three days trying to track down a man named Gus Campagni who said he had an urgent need to speak to me. Mrs. Plaut has assured me that Gus Campagni had been most insistent on the phone, saying that it involved money. Gus Campagni turned out to be the gas company trying to get me to pay the gas bill for an apartment I had lived in three years earlier.

"You are not agile," Mrs. Plaut observed as I managed to reach out and stop my fall with my right hand while I pulled up my pants with the left. My right shoulder twinged.

"I am not agile," I agreed. "But I bounce easily."

"The telephone waits," she reminded me as I crossed the room in search of a shirt. I paused, shrugged, felt the stubble on my face, tasted the tin on my cratered tongue, and shuffled toward the door scratching my stomach and not feeling much like Clark Gable. Mrs. Plaut two-stepped out of my path, mop held high.

No one was on the landing. I glanced toward the door of the room next to mine but remembered that Gunther had told me he would be up early for a meeting with a publisher. Gunther Wherthman, all three feet plus of him, is a Swiss little person who makes a living translating books and articles from any of seven languages into English or each other if the need arises. Gunther is also my best friend and a small cherrystone of sanity in a world made of Jell-O. I shuffled toward the phone near the stairs knowing Mrs. Plaut was close behind.

"Following your conversation, I would like a brief discussion," she said.

"Urggkh," I grunted and picked up the dangling phone. "Peters," I croaked.

"Toby?" came the voice of Sheldon Minck, D.D.S., with whom I share office space.

"There is no other Peters at this address, Shel," I said irritably. "It's seven in the morning. I just . . ."

"She's missing, Toby," he cried. When I say "he cried," I mean exactly that. I could imagine the tears running down his Kewpie cheeks, could picture the thick glasses sliding toward the end of his sweating nose, could see his hairless head catching the reflection of light from the always sputtering light bulb in the ceiling of his office.

"Take the cigar out of your mouth, Sheldon," I said.

"Sorry," he said. "I'm just so . . . so . . ."

". . . early," I supplied. "It's seven in the morning."

"Mildred's missing," he wept.

"Missing," I repeated, glancing over at Mrs. Plaut, who was no more than a foot away, cocking her head like a sparrow.

"Missing, gone, disappeared," he said. "Run away."

"Run away," I said, looking at Mrs. Plaut, who nodded knowingly. I wondered what the hell she thought was going on.

"If you're just going to repeat everything I say," bleated Shelly, "we're never going to find her."

Mildred Minck was about Shelly's age, fifty-five or so, spike-thin, hard of face and heart, and given to wearing clothes too young for her. She wore her hair piled high, pointing toward the sky like a lacquered ack-ack gun. She was a screecher who thought I was a bad influence on Shelly, and she kept her steel fingers on the family checkbook.

"You want me to find Mildred," I said.

"Brilliant," he laughed sarcastically. "The man is brilliant. I know I've come to the right man. A detective who . . ."

"Shelly," I said feeling Mrs. Plaut's jasmine tea breath on my neck.

"OK, OK. When I came home from New York last night, she wasn't there. I thought she might have gone to her sister's."

"Abigail, Queen of the Valkyries," I said.

"That's unkind," he whined.

"It's what you call her, Shel," I reminded him. "I've never met the woman. I've never met anyone in her family or in yours. I've never been invited to your house."

"It's still unkind," he said. "So, I just went to bed and this morning I found the note here at the office. She's run off with Peter Lorre."

"Peter Lorre?" I said.

I turned to Mrs. Plaut, who mouthed "Peter Lorre" silently.

"They've run off together. It says right here in the note, for God's sake."

He crinkled the note into the phone in evidence. It sounded like the noise they make for fire on radio shows.

"I'm sorry, Shel, but . . ."

"And she took all the money, everything we had in the bank, everything but my secret nest egg in the Buddha. And you know what plans I had for Mildred's and my money," he whimpered.

"Electric teeth cleaning, colored false teeth," I said.

"That's just part of . . . It's not the money, Toby. Not the money at all. Mildred is . . . I love Mildred."

Mrs. Plaut's face was so close now it was almost between me and the receiver. I turned to her and said, "He loves her."

"He loves Peter Lorre?" she asked in wide-eyed astonishment.

"No, his wife. . . ."

"Toby, who the hell are you talking to? The world's falling apart and you're fooling around there. I can't think."

"I'm on my way, Shel," I said.

"Stop by Smokey Al's and pick up two of those big Danish cinnamon rolls and a large coffee with double cream," Shelly added.

"I don't want a Danish," I said.

"They're both for me," he said. "God, I'm so upset I can't even make myself understood here."

Before I could get involved in further pathos or get knocked over by Mrs. Plaut, who was close enough to take a bite out of the phone, I hung up and moved back.

"Rubber, Mr. Peelers," she said.

"Right, Mrs. P.," I said with my best unwinning toothy smile as I backed toward my room.

"A nation-wide campaign to collect scrap rubber was announced this very morning by President Franklin Delano Roosevelt."

"I appreciate your letting me know, Mrs. Plaut," I said backing into my room with the black-smocked demon in close pursuit.

"It will last two weeks and all Americans are expected to participate," she said. "I heard that on the Blue Network."

"Then it must be true," I said, opening my closet door in the hope of finding a clean shirt with all the buttons. There was no such shirt.

"Rubber, fats, and grease," she said. "They'll be collected at gasoline stations. The army and the navy need rubber."

"And grease," I reminded her, scanning the floor for the shirt I must have worn the day before. I found it partially draped over one of my shoes and partially lying under the other. I held it up.

"Throw it away," Mrs. Plaut advised. I shrugged, considered the alternatives, and put on the shirt. Maybe I'd get a chance to pick up a couple of shirts at Hy's Clothes for Him on Hollywood.

I needed a shave but I wasn't going to stop for one, not because of Shelly's cry for help and Danish cinnamon rolls, but a sudden urgent need to escape before I learned more about scrap rubber and grease than might be healthy for me. I slipped on my shoes and I grabbed a tie from my closet without looking closely to see if it matched my trousers or the gray poplin jacket on the door handle.

"Things needed," Mrs. Plaut said, pursing her lips in disapproval as I turned fully dressed to her for response, "include soap dishes, sink plugs, pencil erasers, headless dolls, old pairs of galoshes."

"How about a dish scraper or a faucet spray?" I chimed in, heading for the door again.

"Yes," she agreed. "Or preserve jar rings."

"A window wedge," I contributed.

We were beginning to sound like a grotesque version of Astaire and Rogers doing a Cole Porter song. Mrs. Plaut barred my way, mop at the ready.

"Or the mutilated rubber bone of Mr. Tortelli's dog Mitzi," she said triumphantly.

"That too," I agreed.

"We just take it all to your friend at the garage."

"No-neck Arnie is not interested in legal patriotism," I said.

"We just take it all to your friend at the garage," she repeated, "and he gives us one cent a pound for all contributions."

"I have nothing rubber to donate," I said. "I am fresh out of rubber. Had I a supply of rubber I would gladly give it without the bounty. I am as patriotic as the next guy."

"No," she said, shifting to block an inside move by me toward the door. "The next guy is Albert Tortelli and he is unwilling to give up any of the items including that dog bone, which particularly galls me in view of the needs of our armed forces men and women throughout the world."

"I too am galled," I said. "Now I've got to go."

"Peter Lorre can wait. He is Japanese."

There was no response to such a statement. Knowing Mrs. Plaut, an answer would only take us into a dark closet of conversation where the echoes would reverberate endlessly and meaninglessly till I strangled her or ran in helpless panic.

"What do you want me to do, Mrs. Plaut?" I said in surrender.

"You are to confront and convince Mr. Albert Tortelli that he must give up that rubber bone. I am giving up my preserve jar rings. He refuses to listen to me or to President

Franklin Delano Roosevelt. I'm sure Fala has given up his rubber bone."

"I'm sure," I said. "I'll talk to Mr. Tortelli as soon as I get back home."

"As soon as you return?"

"The very instant," I said.

"As a publisher and exterminator you come into contact with the public and certainly have to be most persuasive," she said, beaming in truimph and finally explaining. "Mr. Tortelli will be oatmeal in your hands."

"A charming image," I said making my way through the door and toward the stairs.

If by chance you are confused by Mrs. Plaut's belief that I am an editor and exterminator, try to accept it as I have. It is easier. When you unwind a ball of string, you don't come to the meaningful core. You end up with empty air. So, too, with attempting to understand Mrs. Plaut.

I escaped down the stairs, touching my stubbled face, running my tongue over my gravelly teeth, and burst onto the porch. Heliotrope was silent at this hour except for Mr. Tortelli's dog next door who was whining either because he was in great need of a favorite curb or because he sensed that, later in the day, Toby Peters was coming for his beloved bone.

2

There were plenty of parking spaces at seven-thirty and my Crosley didn't need a very big one. I parked on Hoover about a block from the Farraday, eased myself out of the car, and walked quickly down the street. I wasn't in a hurry to see Shelly even though the paper bag I held away from my body was leaking.

I elbowed into the Farraday's lobby taking in the ever present smell of Lysol our landlord Jeremy Butler dosed the place with. The Farraday was relatively quiet as I listened to my footsteps echo on the tile floor and bypassed the elevator to head up the stairs. The elevator worked. It just didn't work very quickly. I put one hand under the soaked sack while the other grasped its top as I took the steps two at a time. Somewhere on the second floor someone, male or female, either screamed or yawned or called a name. I kept going. By ten that morning a simple scream would be one of the more reassuring sounds in the Farraday, whose tenants included a shyster, several quacks, various frauds, a petty pornographer, two fortune tellers, three one-room "schools" for whatever was hot that day, a baby photographer, an unsuccessful loan shark, a dentist, a poet-landlord, and a private detective named Toby Peters who now stood in front of the door bearing his name in black letters on pebbled glass just below that of "Sheldon Minck, D.D.S., S.D., D.R.L."

My hand was sticky, warm, and wet. I pushed open the door, kicked it closed behind me, ignored the mess in the small outer waiting room and opened the door to Shelly's office. He was sitting where I expected him to be, in his dental chair. His nose twitched, pushing his glasses back a fraction of an inch. His pudgy hands were crossed on his stomach over a wrinkled white smock. His cigar drooped unlit in his mouth and he looked up at me near tears.

"Look around," he said. "What do you see?"

I saw a mess of an office, dirty instruments piled on the tray next to the chair on top of a copy of *Collier's* magazine. I saw, in the corner, a sink filled with coffee cups and small dishes. The water was dripping. I saw Shelly's instrument cabinet with some of the drawers open. I saw the door to my cubbyhole office partly open. The place looked the way it always looked.

"I see a mess," I said.

He looked at me sadly and shook his head in sorrow.

"No," he said. "You see a meaningless space. An empty space. The inside of an abandoned shell. Toby, if you could see inside of me . . ." With this he pointed to his chest to let me know where I would have to look if I could but see inside him. "If you could see inside me, you would see the same emptiness."

I opened the bag in my hand, pulled out a dripping container of coffee, and handed it to him.

"Fill some of the emptiness with this and tell me what happened," I said.

He put his cigar on the end of the nearby work table and reached up halfheartedly to take the coffee.

"Danish?" he asked.

I handed him a Danish. He balanced the coffee in one hand, the damp Danish in the other. There was something wrong with the scale.

"I asked for two," he said, biting the coffee-sogged roll.

"Contain your grief," I said, pulling out the other roll and placing it on a semiclean space on the *Collier's* right next to a slightly rusted metal pick.

"Food helps," he said, and washed down a mouthful of Danish with a gulp of coffee. He made a face. "This isn't triple sugar?"

"Double sugar," I said, throwing the soaked bag toward the already filled metal trash basket near the dental chair. I missed. The sack landed right next to a crumpled cloth which was dry and bloody.

Shelly sighed. First his wife had run away with a movie actor and now he had to endure coffee without a triple sugar. Life was not only tragic. It was unfair.

I went to the sink and rinsed my sticky hands under the dripping faucet. Behind me Shelly ate noisily and sighed between gulps. When I turned, my own coffee in hand, the first Danish was gone and he had started on the second.

"That woman is a saint, Toby," he said, chewing slowly. "A saint. Like . . . a saint."

"Shel," I said, pulling out the stool he usually sat on when he attacked natives foolish enough to walk into his dental trap. "What makes you think Mildred has run away with Peter Lorre?"

I sat on the stool, sipped my tepid coffee, and wondered when I was going to get to shave. Shelly grunted and nodded toward the small table. His pudgy cheeks jiggled. His nose twitched. He finished his second Danish and looked at his fingers in the hope that something had somehow clung to them, something worth eating. I followed his nod and got off the stool. Sticking out of the magazine was an envelope. I took it, finished my coffee, tossed the empty container toward the garbage (missed again), and pulled a single sheet of white linen paper from the envelope.

"Look at the outside. Look at what it says," the myopic dentist said, pointing at the envelope.

"It says, 'Dear Sheldon.'"

"Dear Sheldon," he repeated forlornly, leaning forward. "She still has feeling for me, Toby."

"You're sure it's her writing?" I asked.

"Am I . . . did Napoleon know Josephine's handwriting?" he asked.

"I don't know," I said. "Did he?"

Shelly sank back.

I read the note aloud: "'Dear Sheldon: I am with Peter Lorre, the actor. . . .'"

"How many Peter Lorres are there, for Chrissake?" he moaned.

I went on reading. "'We are in love. It can't be helped. It is bigger than both of us.'"

"That's not hard," Shelly mumbled. "The guy's nothing but a bug-eyed dwarf. She left me for a bug-eyed Italian dwarf."

"I think he's German or Hungarian or something," I said. "You want me to finish reading this, or do you want to spend the next day or two interrupting?"

"Go on," he moaned.

"'I've taken most of my things,'" I read. "'I'll send for the rest. You'll hear from my lawyer about the divorce. Don't forget to clean up the office. Love, Mildred Evangeline Minck.'"

"Love," Shelly sighed loudly. "What am I going to do without her, Toby? What? You've lost a wife. Tell me."

I found it impossible to compare Anne's walking out on me to Mildred's abandonment of Shelly. There was probably a lot to compare. I just couldn't bring myself to do it. I didn't answer.

"What do you want from me, Shel?" I said with what I hoped had the sound of sympathy. "I brought the Danish and coffee. I've heard your story. Now you've got to start living with it. There are things you'll learn to like."

"Never," he said, standing up and sending a spray of Danish crumbs to the floor from the lap of his dirty smock. "I want you to find her, find them. I want to talk to her in person. I want to know she's all right, that he hasn't hypnotized her or something. Toby, I think he's after her money. I really do."

"It's a possibility," I agreed. Actually, it seemed the only possibility, though I didn't know why an apparently successful actor would need money and a possible scandal. My imagination has been praised by the police and bad guys, actors and bums, but I couldn't come up with a plausible picture of the person who would want to spend a life of love with Mildred Minck.

"I had such plans, Toby," Shelly said, looking around the room. The only worthwhile plans I could think of for the space would involve total demolition. "Without Mildred . . . it doesn't seem worthwhile."

And without Mildred's money, it, whatever it was, wouldn't even be possible.

"OK. So I find her. What then?"

"Nothing," he said showing his palms to make it clear that he was concealing nothing. "A simple talk, an opportunity to discuss it. I just want to know she's all right, that he didn't. . . ."

". . . hypnotize her," I finished.

"It's possible," he said.

"Ten bucks a day plus expenses," I said, running my palm across my stubbled face.

Shelly looked at me, puzzled.

"Ten bucks . . . are you saying? Are you telling me you're going to charge me?" Shelly said pointing at himself.

"Ten bucks a day plus expenses," I said. "That's my rate for friends."

"I can't believe this," Shelly looked up and told the ceiling. "My best friend, my closest . . . in my time of torment. Would I charge you for dental work? Have I ever charged you for dental work?"

"I've never wanted you to work on my teeth," I said. "If I'm ever drunk enough to let you, feel free to charge me. I'll deserve it. Maybe it'll teach me to stay sober. You charge me rent for the closet, don't you?"

"But that's different," Shelly whimpered, retrieving his cigar. "That's business."

"And looking for Mildred is pleasure?"

"Five dollars and no expenses," he said.

"Ten and you clean this place up," I said. "Today."

"Clean it. . . ?" he asked, looking around the room.

"It's what Mildred wants," I said, holding up the letter.

He sank back in his chair giving me the look of one betrayed, which I was sure was meant to make me feel the guilt.

"No charge for the coffee and Danish," I said. "I'll be in my office. You think about it."

I stopped at the sink, turned on the hot water, waited for about thirty seconds while it got hot, rinsed out a coffee cup from the pile of dirty dishes and filled it from the tap. I turned off the dripping water, knowing it would start again by the time I was seated in my office. With my free hand I grabbed the soap and one of Shelly's towels, reasonably clean, and went into my office, closing the door behind me.

There was a pile of mail on my desk but I had something more urgent to do. I sat down, glanced down through my window at the alley behind the Farraday, opened my desk drawer and pulled out the Gillette safety razor I kept there for emergencies. I took out the rusty blade and put a fresh one in. The sun was up and I couldn't make out my face in the window. Using the cup of warm water and the bar of soap, I shaved. My office was barely large enough for my desk, my chair and one chair for a client, though I did my best not to meet clients in my office. It wasn't just that Shelly tried to trap them into orthodontia before they made it to my door. A look around my office made it a little tough to convince the client of my success.

I looked at my framed State of California license, the old dusty photograph on the wall of me when I was a kid, my dad with one arm around me, one arm around my brother Phil. In front of us sat Kaiser Wilhelm, our dog.

When I finished shaving and started to wipe the soap from my face, Shelly opened my door without knocking. His head floated in like a bespectacled beach ball.

"It shouldn't take you long to find her, should it?" he asked.

"If she's really with Peter Lorre, it shouldn't take long," I said.

He contorted his face in something resembling thought.

"OK," he said. "Ten dollars a day."

"Plus expenses," I reminded him.

"You've got soap on your nose," he said, and closed the door.

Shelly could have done what I did next. I picked up the phone, called Warner Brothers studios, and asked for security. The guy who answered said his name was Lyons. I didn't know Lyons. I asked for Mike or Bill Durban. I had worked in security for the brothers Warner till '38 when Jack Warner got upset after I gave one of his B-movie cowboy stars a nose almost as flat as mine. The cowboy, whom I was supposed to be guarding, made an unpleasant comment about the origin of an actress. I'd asked him to shut up. I'd asked him very politely. There was a Depression on. I was married and I didn't want to lose my job but there are some things a man just can't avoid stepping into. Jack Warner didn't see it that way when his cowboy star missed four days in front of the camera after I flattened his nose. The Durban brothers had been at the studio almost as long as the Warners. I had the feeling the Durbans would have made better producers too.

"Durban," came a raspy voice.

"Peters," I said. "Mike?"

"Mike, right," he said. "How you been, Toby? Heard you were counting stacks of green, living off the fat, that kind of stuff. Heard you did a job for Cooper a while back. Me and Bill been thinking of striking out on our own."

I didn't believe him, but I wanted a favor.

"You'd probably do better than I'm doing, Mike. I still have to fill in as a night-shift house dick here and there."

"Hell, Toby, maybe there's no easy money," he sighed.

"You can always go in front of the cameras."

"What do you mean, could? Bill and I are filling in all over the place. Young guys, extras are off killing Japs or Krauts. Director sees us holding down a door and right away they put us in a cowboy suit or a gangster pinstripe. Even played a postal clerk a few weeks back."

"That's a fact?" I said.

"It gets us a few extra bucks but it's not our line," he said. "We are not acting material. If we could lop off a few years, Bill and I would be out there on some island in the Pacific. Bill's a shot, he is. You remember."

"He's a shot, Mike," I said.

"We'll maybe tip an ale to the past if you make it this way," he said. "But that wasn't on your mind this day."

"Peter Lorre," I said. "Is he working a picture with you? Or do you have a number on him?"

"He was here back at Christmas. Something like *All Through the Night,* but I hear he's over at Universal on something. Nice man. Took Bill for eight bucks and some change at poker one noon before he took off. Nice man though. You want a number, you say?"

He gave me a home number and I asked him what he knew about Lorre.

"Know? Some kind of German or something. Wouldn't think it to look at him but the little fella's a bit of a lady's man. Got a wife but there was this woman, another German, in the picture and they seemed to be getting on pretty good. This the kind of thing you want?"

Beyond the closed door of my office I heard the outer door open and Shelly's professional voice, about two octaves lower than normal, greeting a potential victim.

"That's the kind of thing I want," I said.

"You ask me," Mike said lowering his voice. "There're too damned many Germans at the studio. Directors, actors, camera guys. There's a war, you know."

"I know, Mike. Anything else you can tell me?"

The pause was short and I could hear his labored breathing as he hesitated and then sighed a what-the-hell sigh.

"Bill and I hear they're going to offer Lorre a contract here, but keep it under your fedora. Nothing like what the big boys are getting but maybe seventeen hundred and fifty a week with a two-, maybe three-picture guarantee."

"Thanks, Mike," I said as Shelly's drill began to whine in the next room. "We'll have that ale soon."

He laughed. "When the Yanks roll into Berlin."

"Why not?"

I hung up, looked at the phone number, and listened to Shelly singing a mournful version of "Lulu's Back in Town" to the accompaniment of the electric drill. He didn't sound exactly happy but he was doing what he liked best. I called the number Mike Durban had given me and listened to the phone ring seven times before someone picked it up. The instant a woman's voice answered, Shelly's drilling stopped.

"Yes?"

"Is Mr. Lorre in?" I asked.

"No, may I ask who is calling?" Her voice had more than a trace of Europe.

"Arnold Sapir, Warner Brothers," I said. "It's important that I find him immediately."

"Arnold . . ."

"Sapir," I said. "I really must talk to him before . . ."

And Shelly's drill burst into song along with Shelly doing a loud but somber imitation of Nelson Eddy singing "Shortnin' Bread."

"I can't hear . . ." she began.

I put my hand over the mouthpiece of the phone and shouted out to Shelly to be quiet. He stopped suddenly. Into

He smelled of overly sweet aftershave, but Carmen, ah Carmen, smelled of Jewish food and voluptuous fantasies.

"Toby," she said, glancing at me and then back to the change she was counting, "haven't seen you for a few days."

"Weeks, Carmen, weeks. I was in New York. Government case," I whispered past the toothpick muncher, who took his change and looked at me. I held a finger to my lips to indicate that as a loyal American he should keep silent about what he had just heard. "Loose lips," I said to him.

The man nodded, belched, and walked off.

"I was shot in the arm saving Albert Einstein," I said to Carmen quietly. It wasn't quite true but it was close enough. I rolled up my sleeve to show her the bandage. She looked politely and reached back to turn on the radio. Singing Sam's deep voice came on, telling us it was Coca Cola Refreshment Time and that he was going to sing both "What Do You Hear from Your Heart?" and "The Night We Met in Honolulu," both of which he proceeded to do while I finished my minibarrage on Carmen, who hummed along and, with the help of a small hand mirror, examined her large, white teeth for lipstick stains.

"Shot," I said. "In the arm."

She looked up again in the general direction of my arm but with no great curiosity.

"Shot," she repeated. "Einstein shot you in the arm? Frankly Toby, no offense, but I don't believe you."

"Would you believe dinner on Saturday and Show Time at the Biltmore, buck-fifty tickets," I said, flush with the recent advance from Shelly.

"Who's playing?" Carmen asked cautiously.

"Vaudeville," I said leaning over the counter to confide my secret. "Georgie Jessel, Jack Haley, Ella Logan, Kitty Carlisle, and the DeMarcos."

"Saturday?" she asked, large brown eyes careful, checking for a lie.

"Saturday," I said. "I'll pick you up and I'll wear a clean shirt."

3

Levy's ran a special on Wednesday afternoons. Choice of brisket, liver and onions, or chicken with vegetable, coffee, and vanilla ice cream for thirty-two cents. I had tried them all more than once. I wasn't exactly a regular at Levy's but I came frequently enough for assaults on Carmen, the dark, exotic, and slightly hefty beauty who cashiered behind the counter on a wooden stool. Since chance had led me to Levy's, I decided to seize the opportunity and plead my case again with the cashier of my dreams.

On more than one occasion I had managed to put together a semimatching clean jacket, trousers, shirt, and tie, lather my scuffed shoes, and convince Carmen that the night of her dreams was in store for her if she would but accompany me to the movies or a boxing card at Madison Square Arena. Carmen was a challenge. The world bored her. Her dreams, if she had any, were her own and buried deep inside that ample body. My dream was simple, to bury myself in Carmen for at least one night of ecstasy. Carmen didn't smell of perfume. She smelled of corned beef, new dill pickles, copper pennies and an additional faint scent of woman. She was an enigma who preferred wrestling to boxing, Tony Martin to Bing Crosby, certified public accountants to me.

I hadn't seen Carmen in about two weeks. I'd been busy in New York.

"Carmen," I whispered over the head of an egg-shaped man with a toothpick in his mouth who was trying to pay his bill.

"Your car . . ." she began as a pair of late-lunch customers hurried toward her, checks in hand.

"It's clean, no more camouflage colors. I explained that. Believe . . ."

She reached for the check of a pencil-shaped man whose neck was wrinkled under a starched collar.

"Six o'clock, my apartment. Sit-down restaurant with tables," she said, looking away. "No taco place with stools like last time. No hot dogs at Manny's."

"Sit-down table," I agreed. "Real food." The pencil-shaped man didn't care. He took his change, put a finger inside his collar to search for room that wasn't there, and moved on.

"I gotta work," Carmen said reaching brightly painted fingernails for the next customer's check.

"Me too," I said with a wink at the customer who was pulling a buck out to pay his tab. Unfortunately, the customer had a permanently lowered right eyelid and made it clear that if he weren't about five-one and about a hundred pounds he'd ram my already battered face through the glass front of Carmen's cashier's counter.

"You got something to say?" he challenged.

I didn't. I turned away storing the hope of Saturday ecstasy away till I got back to my room at Mrs. Plaut's that night. What dreams of Carmen I would have! But it was time for work and Levy's was not at its busiest.

Finding Peter Lorre was no problem. He sat with his back to the door at a rear table. I could tell it was him from the rear. He was short, his hair slicked down, and a haze of cigarette smoke hung over the table. I could see the man who sat across from him facing the door quite clearly. There was something familiar about his small, intense face and the twisted little black cigar in his mouth. As I made my way to their table I could hear, over Singing Sam in the background, waitresses shouting orders and Lorre and the other man speaking German. I dodged a skinny waitress balancing an armful of hot plates and stood next to the two seated men.

The man with the cigar was the first to notice that I wasn't there to take their order. He said something to Lorre who turned to look up at me over his left shoulder. The actor was wearing a solid white sweater over his white shirt.

Peter Lorre looked younger than I had expected. His face was as unlined as a five-year-old's and his slightly closed eyes and straight black hair falling over his forehead added to the childlike look.

"Yes?" he asked.

"My name's Peters," I said. "Toby Peters. We met a couple of years ago over at Warner Brothers. You were on a break on the *Maltese Falcon* set playing cards."

He smiled up at me politely and took a drag at his cigarette but it was clear that he didn't remember me.

"Well, Mr. . . ."

"Peters," I supplied.

"Yes, Mr. Peters. It is good to meet you again but my friend and I are discussing some business and . . ."

"Mildred Minck," I said. The most striking thing about Lorre was his voice. It was much lower and less accented than I remembered it from seeing and hearing him on the screen. The same thing had struck me when I first met him back at Warners, but there had been so many radio imitations of the famous voice that I had forgotten what the real one sounded like.

Lorre's unlined forehead lined suddenly.

"I beg your pardon," he said.

"Mildred Minck," I repeated.

The man with the cigar asked a question in German and Lorre answered before turning to me to say, "Mildred Minck. You are selling some kind of fur called mildred mink?"

A waitress asked me to sit down because I was in the way so I did without waiting for an invitation from Lorre.

"I'm selling nothing," I said. "I'm looking for Mildred Minck. I'm a private investigator. I'd show my card but I don't have any more. I gave my last one to a woman named

Cleland who was considering hiring me to find her missing cat. That was back in thirty-nine."

The waitress reached over my shoulder to serve Lorre and the other man. Both had the specials. Lorre had the chicken. The other guy had liver and onions. I told the waitress I'd take the brisket.

"Did you find the cat?" Lorre asked with what appeared to be genuine interest.

"She didn't hire me. She was just shopping around."

"Mildred Minck," Lorre repeated. "Am I supposed to have some information about this person?"

"According to a note from her, she ran away with you," I said.

"I ran away with someone named . . ."

"Mildred Minck," the man with the cigar said with a knowing nod.

"Do you have a photograph of Miss Minck?" Lorre said.

"Mrs. Minck," I corrected.

While I fished out the photo I'd removed from Shelly's office, Lorre and the other man dug into their food. I handed Lorre Mildred's picture.

"That is not a flattering photograph," he said, showing it to the other man, who examined Mildred's picture carefully, then shrugged and speared a rectangle of liver.

"Actually, it is," I said putting the picture back in my wallet. "I take it, then, that you don't know Mildred."

"That is correct," Lorre said. "I am a married man and I do not pursue married women. Occasionally a woman other than my wife has shown an interest in me, though I am not a conventional hero as you might well judge from the roles I have played. These women have been, by and large, quite attractive."

"And Mildred . . . ?" I pushed.

"I will not insult another man's wife without cause simply because I am given the opportunity," he said with a mischievous smile.

"I don't see why not," I said. "I do it on a regular basis."
Lorre laughed, translated my words to the other man, who
removed his cigar long enough to let out a choked chortle,
and returned to his meal.

"I've never met a real private detective before," Lorre said.
"You'd think that after playing a Japanese detective and con-
fronting Sam Spade I would have gone out of my way to meet
someone of your profession but I never considered such first-
hand knowledge necessary. Do you solve murders and get hit
on the head with any frequency?"

Our waitress interrupted with the three specials. My brisket
looked lean and I dug in, talking while I ate.

"I get hit on the head, neck, shoulders, stomach, thighs,
legs, feet, and even the ankles. The ankle attack came from a
feisty midget who later got thrown out of a hotel window," I
said, forking a potato and tucking it neatly into my cheek.

The guy with Lorre said something in German and I caught
what might have been the word "feisty." Lorre explained in
German and then turned to me. "Fascinating."

"Some people have gotten themselves murdered in my
vicinity," I admitted, reaching for a chocolate phosphate that
may have been mine. "I don't know about solving murders.
Sometimes the people who kill get caught. Sometimes they
don't."

The guy with the cigar reached out and snatched the chocolate phosphate. I grinned and chewed.

"We must talk further of this," Lorre said, "but Herr
Brecht and I have some business . . ."

"Right," I said, holding up my hand. "I'll gulp this down,
make a sandwich of the brisket, and get out of your way."

"I don't wish to be rude," Lorre said as I reached past him
for a couple of slices of pumpernickel, "and I'll gladly pay for
your lunch."

"And I'll gladly accept, with thanks." I deposited the brisket between the bread slices and finished off the last of the
potatoes.

"Final question, Mr. Peters," Lorre said. "In case I might

need your services, are you a good detective? I mean can you give me some references?"

"No," I said, "but I'll give you something better than a reference. You're about to get a contract offer from Warner Brothers, about seventeen hundred a week with a three-picture deal."

I took a big bit of my sandwich and grinned down at him.

"Remarkable," he said. "My agent has just confirmed such an offer is coming. In fact Herr Brecht and I are here in anticipation of that offer and the possibility that we might now be able to work together on a film project. Back in Germany, Herr Brecht gave me my first major theater work. In a sense, he discovered me. And . . . but wait, there is a matter of some discretion for which I might well need your services."

The last he whispered.

I leaned forward and with brisket breath said, "The young German lady you met on your last film."

Lorre's jaw dropped. His large, round eyes drooped and the corners of his mouth dipped.

"That's the look in *The Man Who Knew Too Much,* just before you grabbed the girl," I said.

The look on Lorre's face disappeared and he shook his head.

"You are an intriguing man, Mr. Peters, an intriguing man. I think we might be able to do some business. I'm very pleased that you found me."

I stuffed what was left of my sandwich in my mouth, wiped my hands on the napkin near my empty plate, pulled out a gnarled pencil and wrote my name and phone number on the list of today's specials.

"I'm sorry I could not be of more help," Lorre said with a shrug, finally reaching for a fork. Brecht had eaten through the whole encounter, finished his chicken, and started a fresh cigar, though I don't think the twisted black things he was smoking could ever have been fresh.

"Hey," I said, "you eliminated yourself as a suspect."

We pitched a little small talk back and forth, movies, the

war, and the private detective business. Lorre told me about a movie he and his friend Brecht wanted to do about a man who comes home and finds a stranger locked in his closet.

"You never see the stranger," Lorre said, "just me, the man who comes home. I try to coax him out, but he won't come."

Brecht said something in German.

"Yes, that's right," agreed Lorre. "We would get someone with a name to do the voice of the person in the closet. We could probably get someone very good for very little money because they wouldn't even have lines to learn. They could sit behind the door and read their lines from the script like a radio show. But there are problems."

"Like who wants to watch a movie with only one man in a room," I said.

"No," said Brecht who seemed to understand more English than he was letting on.

"No," agreed Lorre. "My character would go back out, stop at a diner, meet a woman."

"Sounds fine to me," I said getting up. "But I've got to get going now."

I got up, thanked them for their time, and told Lorre to give me a call if he thought he needed my services.

I tried to catch Carmen's eye as I headed out of Levy's but she was busy juggling cash and trying to find something on the radio. As I headed for the YMCA on Hope Street, I made some plans and digested brisket.

Lorre hadn't run off with Mildred Minck, didn't know where she was, didn't know who had, didn't know anything about it. So, either Mildred was lying, had been forced to write what she wrote, or she really thought she was running off with Peter Lorre. The outright lie seemed the best bet but there was too much wrong with it. Why pick Peter Lorre to lie about? Wouldn't it be more likely that Mildred would claim to be swept off her varicose limbs by Robert Taylor? And wouldn't she know, wouldn't even Mildred Minck know, that it would be as easy as a phone call and a short drive to prove the lie? Next stop: She was forced to write the note. OK. Why would anyone force Mildred Minck to write a note saying she was running off with Peter Lorre? If that was the answer, I was probably lost and would never find her. I'd be dealing with a maniac with a sense of humor unequaled since Bluebeard. Final stop: Mildred thought she had run away with Peter Lorre.

This was getting me somewhere. Los Angeles couldn't be filled with Peter Lorre look-alikes. So, how does one go about finding a Peter Lorre imitator? Talent agencies. I was feeling better by the time I got to the Y. I had a plan, a direction, and a sore arm and tender back. Things were better than normal.

It was an off hour. I didn't expect anyone to be around, at least not many people. There weren't. The guy at the desk whose name was Alf or Ralph, I couldn't remember which, looked up from his newspaper when I came in. He was old, skinny, and wearing a white T-shirt to show his bones. I nodded and he told me that a Japanese sub had torpedoed an American merchant ship off the coast up above San Francisco.

"A fishing boat for Chrissakes," he said, the gray skin on his neck shaking. "Can you imagine?"

"Happened today?" I asked.

"Sunday," he answered absently, seeing into the future or his fears. "Remember back March, April they shelled a tanker right off of Frisco?"

"I remember," I said. "And they shelled Goleta in February. How about a towel?"

He threw me a white towel and shook his head.

"It's getting so . . ." Alf or Ralph started and then paused.

I never found out what it was getting. I went into the locker room, found my locker, got undressed, put on my jock, shorts, socks, gym shoes, and sweat shirt, put on my sweat-stiff leather gloves, and trotted up to the gym. My arm didn't exactly ache, but it let me know that it didn't want any part of this place or what I planned to do. After I'd warmed up with some exercises Doc Hodgdon had given me, a big guy in his late thirties with straight hair that fell over his face like Gene Tunney showed up, gave me a dirty look, and started shadow boxing in a corner of the gym. I made for the punching bag in the corner. The heavy bag dangled next to it. Since the big guy shadow boxing was wearing gloves I figured I'd volunteer to hold the heavy bag for him if he'd do it for me, providing he planned to use it. It was easier than chasing the bag.

"I'll hold the bag for you, you hold it for me," I said.

He grunted, threw me a look of hate, and went on punching shadows.

"Don't mention it," I said and moved to the punching bag.

I'd been working the small bag about five minutes when I felt someone standing over my shoulder. I kept working. My arm was aching now but I had worked up a sweat. I could smell it, feel it. It felt good. I felt good, probably good enough to play a couple of games of handball with old Doc Hodgdon if he happened to be around.

"Hey," the big guy said.

I kept punching and grunted, "Huh?"

"I was on this bag," he said.

I kept punching. I had about two more minutes to do through the pain.

"Be through in . . . two . . . minutes," I grunted.

"You're through now," he said and spun me around by the shoulder. I lost my balance and did a Russian dance going backward to keep from falling. When I knew I wasn't going to go down, I looked at him again. He was big, maybe six-two, a good four inches over me. He also went about 220 pounds to my 180. I was old enough to be his old man, though I might have had to do it fooling around in the back of my father's grocery store in Glendale after high school. The guy stood looking at me, sweat trickling down his smooth chest. I looked at his eyes, his nose, his ears, his body, and I shook my head.

Without catching my breath I walked toward him. He looked mean, angry, much angrier than I had ever seen Tunney. Maybe he had just lost his job. Maybe his wife was giving him a hard time. Maybe he'd just been drafted. Maybe he was just your ordinary, everyday jerk. They're easy to find.

"Step away from the bag, son," I said.

He laughed. There were too many cigarettes in that hacking laugh.

I didn't laugh, just walked up to him, hands at my sides and spoke softly.

"See this face," I said.

He was smirking, ready for me, but he looked at my face, the smashed nose, the scar tissue, and something in my eyes.

"There are more scars on the body if I take off this shirt," I said, "but I'm not going to have to do that. Son, you've never really been hurt. I can see it in your eyes, on your face, your body. You're big and pretty tough, but you don't know what it's like to be hurt. I do. And if you don't back away you are going to learn what being hurt feels like it. I might get hurt a lot more, but I know what it's like."

"You . . ." he began wiping his dangling hair from his face with the back of his hand.

"Hey," I interrupted. "I don't want to talk to you. I don't want to play games with you. I just want to finish my workout and get back to work. So, what'll it be? Do you move away from the bag or do we both get hurt?"

I knew he was moving before he did. I knew it when I took a step past him and his hand didn't go out to grab me again.

"You shit," he muttered.

"When I can, son," I said, "but the older you get, the harder it gets."

I hit the bag and ignored him, or did my best to make it look like I ignored him. I didn't really let myself go on the bag till I heard him stalk across the gym floor and go through the locker room door. As soon as the door slammed, I stopped punching. The pause had stiffened my sore arm and the last minute of punching had been numb agony, but I was sure I felt better than the big guy, who was probably kicking lockers by now and trying to find some way not to admit that a battered middle-aged mug had forced him to admit that he was scared.

All in all, it was a good workout. I didn't look for Doc Hodgdon, couldn't have raised my hand for a game, and I always needed both hands to play the seventy-year-old orthopedist dead even. Hell, I couldn't beat him with two good hands. There was an outside chance that the guy in the gym would talk himself into coming back for me, but it wasn't much of a chance so I didn't worry while I stripped and showered.

On the way out of the gym, I tossed the dirty towel to Ralph or Alf, who caught it and dumped it into the barrel behind him.

"Nimitz really got them," he said to me. "They won't be sending ships back to the coast, right?"

"Not a chance," I agreed. God didn't call me a liar and have the Japanese send a shell through YMCA roof, but I wasn't sure the Battle of Midway had won the war. I didn't think Ralph/Alf was too sure of it either.

"Watch yourself," he called as I headed out. "It's a jungle out there."

"It's a jungle in here," I called back. "It's a jungle no matter where you look."

The sky was clear and free of kamikazes. I got in my Crosley and headed downtown to see a man who might be able to help me find the elusive Mildred Minck.

4

S al Lurtzma's office was on 10th not far from the Farraday, but the building it was in was as far from the Farraday in class as the Brown Derby from Manny's Taco Shack. To begin with, Lurtzma's building didn't even have a name. Every building in downtown Los Angeles has a name, the name of a tree, a fern, the guy who built it, designed it, bought it. Every building, even the decaying last century converted stone mansions and the hurry-up-and-build-them-to-last-a-week brick rectangles.

But Lurtzma was just in a narrow five-story office building with no elevator and three offices on each floor. He was on the fourth floor. I'd been there maybe six, seven times in the last ten years to track someone down.

I parked the Crosley two blocks away in a church parking lot whose concrete was buckled and showed sprigs of weed and grass between the cracks. I got out, opened my trunk, and rummaged through a box of junk for the right sign. I found one about the size of a license plate with the word Deacon printed on it. Alice Pallis, who used to run a pornographic printing business in the Farraday, had made up the cards for me after she went straight and married Jeremy Butler, the Farraday landlord. Alice and Butler were a match made in the Rose Bowl. She could carry a 200-pound printing press in one hand and hold off a cop with the other. In turn, Jeremy, who had not long ago been a professional wrestler, the Terror of Tarzana, could hold Alice in one arm while she held the printing press. I don't think they ever really tried that trick but I was confident they could do it.

But I digress. I put the Deacon sign inside the front windshield and locked the door so no one could steal the sign. Then I ambled the few blocks to Lurtzma's office building. Sal had once been fat. Once wasn't all that long ago. People still referred to him as Fat Sal, but he was fat no longer. The first time I saw him after he had dropped from 400 to anemic I asked what had happened. I should have said he looked good when I asked, but it wouldn't have been true. At 400 he looked like a tomato with a white cotton ball of hair where the stem should be. At 145 he looked like a wrinkled broom whose bristles had gone limp and white. He should have stopped somewhere between.

"I lost a lot of weight," he had explained.

"Right," I had said, seeing that he had no intention of explaining the miracle.

Some said he had gone through a terrible illness and recovered just when it looked as if he were going to join the great talent agents of the past in the waiting room outside God's office.

"I've got a guy for you, God," Sal would say when he got in to see the Big Producer, "a guy who can play an angel better than Freddie Bartholomew. Trust me. Try him. Have I ever steered you up the wrong avenue?"

Others, particularly a lounge singer named Claire, claimed that Sal had lost the weight for love of both sisters in a singing act, Carlotta and Maria Escondera. Anyway, according to Claire, Sal had lost the pounds to get into the competition for the girls. I don't know the outcome—if Claire was right—but I did know that Sal was not married to Carlotta, Maria, or anyone else.

I stopped in front of the fourth-floor door marked Sal Lurtzma, Talent. I knocked. I heard something inside. I knocked again. Nothing. I opened the door and walked in. Sal was behind his desk in his sweat-stained white shirt, sleeves rolled up to show freckled arms covered with white hair. He was talking on the telephone with his back to the door. Standing next to him, leaning forward, was a thin, hawkfaced man with a balding head and sad eyes. The hawkfaced man was dressed entirely in black, jacket, slacks, even the shirt, socks, and shoes. On his stiffly held right wrist sat a green and red parrot, head tilted as if he were listening carefully to Sal's conversation.

The bird was the first to notice me. I stepped in and closed the door. Sal's voice rose, paused, rose higher, complained, cajoled. Sal's desk was piled high with photographs of actors, copies of *Variety*. The chairs in front of the desk and the one lounge against the wall were vintage stuff, ready to give up. But Sal was never ready to give up on a client, hadn't given up on one in the fifty years he had been in the business. The walls were covered, top to bottom, with photographs of clients, some of them dating back to 1900, but one looked in vain, as I had a few times waiting for Sal on the phone, to find a single face or name the local barber would recognize. Sal specialized in losers. I sat on the lounge and waited. Listening to Sal on the phone was an experience.

"Because he can," Sal insisted on the phone. "He can. I say he can. You can hear that he can. Do I lie? Does Sal Lurtzma lie? Have you ever known me to . . . no, no, no. That was not a lie, Celeste. I beg to differ with you on that one. It was not lie. It was an error on my part. He looked much taller in my office, much taller. Yes . . . well, who knows? But other than that, have I ever given you cause to think I was not telling you the complete truth about a . . . that's not fair, Celeste. I thought we were never going to mention them. I really thought they were three sisters. I did. They looked like sisters, didn't they? Two of them were cousins and the third was a boy, not a man, a boy. Well, if you're going to dredge up the past and not listen you're going to miss an act like you've never seen or heard. OK. All right. So you don't believe. How about I put him on the phone? Yes, right now. Why not? Here he is."

Sal put his hand over the mouthpiece and swiveled in his chair to face the man in black and the bird. He also spotted me, rolled his eyes, and mouthed "Wait." Then he said to the man: "Put the bird on the phone."

"The phone?" the man asked with a decided European accent I couldn't place.

"The phone, Edgar, the phone, the phone," Sal whispered hoarsely and then, into the phone, said, "He'll be on in a second, Celeste, just a second." Hand back over the mouthpiece and addressing Edgar, Sal said, "Have him do Zasu Pitts, or what was that other one?"

"Patsy Kelly?" Edgar tried.

"Whichever," Sal said impatiently, holding up the phone.

Edgar shrugged his thin shoulders, whispered something in the parrot's ear and held him out next to the phone. The bird looked at the phone, looked at Sal, looked at me, pecked at the mouthpiece.

"Talk, talk, or you're Guatemalan lunch," Sal said.

"I'll not allow that you speak in that manner," Edgar said indignantly.

"Sorry, sorry," sighed Sal, who turned to me with an even deeper sigh and a glance at bird and man to let me see what trials he had to go through for his clients.

The bird gawked and then, quite clearly, albeit with an accent very much like Edgar's, said, "I really must do my hair. I really must."

Sal's hand shot over the mouthpiece and the bird pecked at it.

"I said Zasu Pitts or Patsy Kelly," he hissed at Edgar. "Not Hepburn. Everybody does Hepburn. Shit."

"Bad bird," Edgar said to the bird, but the bird didn't seem to care.

The Hepburn imitation had stunk, but at least I knew it was supposed to be Hepburn. On the phone again Sal, sweat trickling down his forehead, his white hair a fluff of madness, said, "Well Celeste? Yeah, sure . . . I, but it's a bird for Chrissake, a bird, not Dennis Day. How do you know it was . . . you take my word it's a bird. What do you think it is, a goddamn gorilla? No . . . wait. I'm sorry. It's a bird. A bird. . . . Because the guy who taught him has an accent. I know Kate Hepburn doesn't have an accent. Yeah, his Zasu Pitts has an accent. They all have accents. I don't know. I don't know, Celeste, I'll have to ask."

Hand over the mouthpiece again and again addressing Edgar, "Can he do Maurice Chevalier, Jean Gabin?"

Edgar emphatically shook his head in the negative. Near defeat, Sal returned to Celeste on the phone.

"He can't do Chevalier or Gabin, Celeste. What do you want me to do? Right. No, Edgar's not a ventriloquist. I don't handle ventriloquists anymore. You know that. You will? You do? You can? Wonderful Celeste. Wonderful . . . of course . . . my guarantee . . . my word . . . my reputation. They'll be right over. Make it twenty minutes tops. So, what can I say? I'm sending you a gold mine."

Sal hung up and turned suddenly in his chair with a wet smile on his red face. His nose came within attack distance of the bird, who took a shot at him. Sal pulled his head back and almost fell over.

"Edgar," he said through closed teeth. "I got you an audition for you with Celeste Malmgren at Columbia." He pulled a sheet of paper from the mess on his desk and scribbled something furiously. "Here's the address. Get right over there. They're looking for novelty acts for a short. They're shooting it in color. Can you paint what's-his-name's wings pink or something? It'd help."

Edgar stood erect and with his free hand reached over to stroke the bird, which accepted the hand with closed eyes.

"She is a she, Mr. Lurteesma," Edgar said with dignity. "Her name is Jeanette. And I do not paint her wings." He took the address from Sal and held his arm down to the open-

doored cage so Jeanette could jump in. Jeanette didn't hesi-
tate. She hopped through the door onto a perch and leaned
back to pull the cage door shut with her beak.

"A suggestion, Edgar," Sal said. "Teach her to do some
male actors or cartoon characters. You know what I mean? I
mean, you know, who the hell knows if a parrot is a male or a
female?"

"I know," Edgar said with a smirk. "Jeanette knows."

"Right," Sal said shaking his head. "And other parrots
know. Good luck."

Edgar picked up the cage, glanced at me, looked back at
Sal, and said, "We thank you."

"A day that will live in infamy," Jeanette said.

"That was Roosevelt," Sal said, standing as Edgar moved
around the desk and past me toward the door. "Roosevelt.
Roosevelt's a goddamn man."

"I did not teach her that," Edgar said, "and I will not en-
courage her, what you say, confusion gender."

From the coat rack in the corner, Edgar retrieved a black
hat, perched it on his head, and left the office.

"Peters," Sal said to me, pulling out a crumpled handkerchief to wipe his brow, neck, hair, "take my advice. Stay
away from animal acts."

"I try to, Sal," I said.

"They're stupid and they smell, even the little ones," he
said shaking his head and glaring at the door through which
Edgar and Jeanette had recently passed.

"I've noticed that, Sal," I sympathized.

"And they die young," he added.

"They can't help it, Sal," I said.

"I know that, I know," he said pulling himself together.
"Right, now what can I do for you?"

"Usual fee?" I asked.

"Cash up front," he said. "A man's got to eat, even if it's
only Shredded Ralston."

Since Shredded Ralston was one of my favorite foods, I

said nothing on the subject and went to the heart of the matter.

"Peter Lorre," I said.

Sal sighed a Sal sigh. "Look around. How long have you known me? You think I handle Peter Lorre? I got a realistic view of myself here and no damn view from the window."

With that he got up to look out the window before turning back to me. His suit was crumpled.

"Not the real Peter Lorre," I explained. "Imitators. Either ones you handle or know about."

"You making a joke?" he asked. He then informed the pictures on one wall. "He's making a joke." Then back to me. "This town is up to its ass in Peter Lorre imitators. Everyone does Peter Lorre and Jimmy Durante, and Jean Sablon. Hell, I should have asked Edgar if the damn bird could do Jean Sablon. I've got Jimmy Stewarts, Clark Gables and more Bette Davises than you'd need in a lifetime."

"I don't need Bette Davises," I said sweetly, still seated on the lounge. "I need someone who looks like Lorre, enough like Lorre to maybe fool someone."

"Oh," said Sal, rubbing his hands together and then looking at them to see if the rubbing had created something magic. "I thought you were talking voice. Hell, I've got two who are pretty good, not great, but pretty good."

"I probably want a great one," I said.

"Great I don't have," Sal said, suddenly sad. "I don't get great. I can live without getting great, but . . . wait. Millman. I think it was Millman had a guy who was a dead ringer, or that's what Millman said, but who can trust Millman?"

"Mrs. Millman?" I tried.

"Hah," laughed Sal. "The last person who should trust Millman. I'll give him a call." He picked up the phone, called the operator "honey," and gave her a number.

Sal tapped his fingers on the desk while he waited, picked up a photograph, turned it for me to look at. It was a woman in a turban. She was overly made up. I shrugged. Sal, holding the phone in one hand, looked at the photograph, nodded yes in agreement, and put the photo back on the desk, face down.

"Millman? Lurtzma . . . I can't complain. Just placed a client at Columbia. Looks like multipicture contract . . . this very minute. As God is my witness. I've got another witness right here, a detective. He'll confirm. Peters. Come here. Tell this petzle about Edgar."

I got up, still tight from my workout, and walked to the desk to take the phone.

"Sal just placed a guy named Edgar with Columbia for a short," I said. Sal pulled the phone out of my hand and cackled into it.

"See? What do you mean? Of course he's a detective. Am I doomed today to have no one believe me on the phone? Millman, listen. You had a Peter Lorre mimic who was supposed to be perfect. No, I've got no job for him. I don't want to steal your client. If I had a job I'd want five percent, but I've got no job." Sal fumbled around for a pencil and paper, found them and began to write as he spoke. "I'm pleased . . . I'm delighted . . . just curious. . . . You'll be the first to know. Sal Lurtzma doesn't lie."

He hung up and turned to me.

"What is it with lying in this business?"

"People sometimes exaggerate, Sal," I said. "You are the greatest guy in the world, a rock, but you know it happens."

"Whatever," he said, getting out of his chair and looking out the window again. "I've got some information for you. You want a Squirt? I got no ice."

"No thanks, Sal," I said as he pulled a green bottle from under his desk, pulled an opener out of the drawer, popped the cap, and took a deep drink.

"Hate the stuff but it's good for the belly," he said with a belch. "Guy you might be looking for is named Sidney Kindem. Almost a ringer for Lorre, even uses the professional name Pete R. Lowry. Lots of that going around, but it's usually hootchy-kootchy dancers. Millman says the guy is pretty good. Wouldn't hold up in a face-to-face with the real thing but damn good, know what I mean? There was a guy a few years back, Billy . . . Billy something, looked more like Chaplin than Chaplin, even made some movies. He . . ."

". . . got kicked by an ostrich and died," I finished. "I heard the story. What about this Sidney Kindem?"

Sal thought about getting out of his chair, changed his mind, drank some Squirt, changed his mind, got up, and looked out the window.

"He's working a movie. Small role. Millman didn't handle it. Millman just knows what's what. Small role. Small studio—Miracle. Heard of them?"

"No," I said.

"According to Millman they're shooting on a roof somewhere near Burlington and Beverly. He didn't know which roof."

"I'll find them," I said.

"Could be the wrong Lorre fake," Sal said. "There's a ton of them, but he's the best according to Millman and on that you can trust Millman."

"I'll start there, Sal. Thanks."

I pulled a five out of my cracked wallet and reached over the desk to hand it to him. He tucked it into the sweat-stained pocket of his shirt.

"Got some free news for you, Peters," he added as I stepped toward the door. "There's a guy out there on Grand looking up at the window. I don't think he's getting up his courage to come in and sing a few songs for me. More like he's waiting for you."

"Big guy, straight blond hair, gray zipper jacket, looks a little like Gene Tunney?"

"That's the make and model," Sal agreed.

"We had a little disagreement over at the Y and he followed me here," I said.

"Because you had a disagreement at the Y? That it? People follow you around because of disagreements?"

"Doesn't seem likely, does it?" I said.

"Not to me," Sal said with a shrug and then finished off the last of his Squirt. "But what do I know? I think parrots sound like FDR. Take care of yourself."

"I try, Sal. I try. If this is the wrong Lorre fake . . ." I began.

"My door is always open," Sal said with a grin that revealed teeth so even and nearly white that they certainly weren't his.

On the way out of the building I passed a man and woman bickering. They didn't seem to notice me. I made my way for them by pressing against the wall of the narrow stairway.

"Tenor," said the man with great exasperation. "Tenor, always a tenor." He was thin, wearing a natty sport jacket and a bow tie.

She, just as thin, wore a black dress with a flowered print, and sang, "Baritone. I know a baritone when I hear one. My father was a baritone. My grandfather was a baritone."

"And you're a baritone," said the skinny man as they disappeared above me heading, I assumed, for Sal's office.

The guy from the Y wasn't in sight as I stepped out. If he had been after me to regain his honor, he would have been in front of me, possibly throwing a sucker punch. If he just wanted revenge, he might be waiting back at the car or in the black Ford I had spotted tailing me. Maybe he'd stay with me till he could safely plow into me. But I had the feeling that the guy was after something else, that maybe he hadn't simply picked that day and hour to work out at the Y, that maybe he had followed me there and hurried up to the gym before me to set up the scene. The only problem with that was that I couldn't think of a reason why anyone might want me followed. It would be another two hours before I found out.

Parking was no problem. I found a space just off Beverly on Bonnie Brae. The big guy in the black Ford pulled past me and turned his head away as if he were looking for a street number. One thing was sure. He was new at this. I sat watching till he parked his car half a block down and then I got out and walked backed to Beverly.

On Beverly, not far from Burlington, I went into a narrow diner called Connie's Place. No one was in the place but Connie, a droopy, dark little woman, who stood behind the counter in her white apron smoking and reading the L.A. *Times.* I sat at the counter on one of the eight empty red leatherette-topped stools. Without looking up from her paper, Connie asked, "What can I do you for?"

"Java, two sinkers, and information, Connie," I said.

"Information," said Connie, thinking over the word. "We got the Nips on the run."

"Information about a movie company that's shooting somewhere near here," I said.

Connie put her paper on the counter without folding it and moved to fill a cup with coffee.

"Easy. Half block up Burlington. Eskian's Hardware. They're up on Paul Eskian's roof." She poured the coffee, wiped her palms on her apron, and bare-handed a pair of doughnuts from the glass-covered container behind her.

"Thanks," I said, reaching for the sugar.

"None of my business," Connie said, going back to her paper while I had my coffee and doughnuts, "but there's a guy looking at you through the window. Looks something like that boxer, Tunney—or if he turns his head Bluto in the Popeye cartoons or my husband Lyle if he's looking straight at you. I think he doesn't want to be noticed."

"Which one, Lyle or the guy at the window?"

"Both," she said.

"Thanks," I said dunking one almost stale donut. "I'll watch out for him."

"And I'll keep looking out for Lyle," Connie said, and then added as if it had suddenly dawned on her. "Say, how did you know my name?"

"Lucky guess," I said with a mouthful. "I'm a detective."

"Eighteen cents for the java and jive," she said. "Just leave it on the counter when you go. You know what I don't like about 'Terry and the Pirates'?''

"No, Connie," I said, looking at the reflection of the guy following me in the big soup bowl behind the counter. He did look more like Bluto than Tunney.

"Too many words. The pictures are good but they got so goddamn many words in the balloons you gotta go to college to read the damn thing. Take a look."

She held up the newspaper for me to see.

"See, 'Napoleon,' 'Tarzan,' 'Ella Cinders,' even 'Mary Worth's Family,' which believe me I don't read, don't have words like 'Terry and the Pirates.' It's dumb. He draws these great-looking dames and scrunches them in the corner under the words and makes it all dark."

I grunted in agreement, took the final doughnut in two bites, and finished the coffee. I dropped a quarter on the counter and got up slowly so the clown from the Y could get out of sight.

"See you, Connie," I said.

"Right, next time don't come during rush hour so we can get a chance to chat," she said with a cough.

I walked back to my car with Bluto right behind. In my rearview mirror I watched him run for his Ford. I gave him time, pulled out onto Beverly, and turned on Burlington. There were people on the street heading in and out of stores but it didn't look particularly busy and I didn't see anything that looked like a movie crew. But I had no trouble spotting Eskian's Hardware. I parked in front of it and looked through the window at a balding bear of a man who smiled at me as he pulled a can of paint out of the window.

When I stepped inside, there were a few customers looking at hammers, nails, and pieces of wood. All the customers looked like janitors.

"Can I, I, I help you?" shouted the bear of a man behind the counter. He was wearing a flannel shirt and a big cus-

tomer-is-always-right smile. His stammer wasn't bad enough
to be annoying but you couldn't miss it.

"Yeah," I said. "Connie tells me they're shooting a movie
on your roof."

"On my roof," said the man with a smile looking up at the
ceiling. "Stars and everything. Peter Lorre's up there right
now. On Paul Eskian's roof. Can you, you, you top that? I
haven't had a, a, a look at him. Too busy down here. But, I
mean, can you top that?"

"Wouldn't try," I said. "How do I get up there?"

The smile left the face of the man I assumed was Paul
Eskian.

"Don't know I can let, let, let you do that," he said. "I
don't think they want people watching. Don't even think
they'll take, take, take, take it kindly if I go up there and it's
my roof. But what the hell. They're giving me free, free, free
passes to see the picture when it's finished."

"You're getting paid in passes?" I asked, looking over my
shoulder toward a stack of paint cans in the corner and seeing
Bluto turn away outside the window.

"Passes and eight bucks for the day," said Eskian, his smile
returning. "Mr. and Mrs. Eskian didn't raise fools for children. My son set the whole thing up. Bright, bright, bright
kid. But I don't think I can let, let . . ."

I pulled out my wallet and flashed the Dick Tracy badge my
nephews Nate and Dave had given me. If you looked closely,
you could see Dick's distinct profile embossed in the tin along
with the decoder nob. Nothing but the best for Uncle Toby.
Eskian didn't look close.

"Sorry," he said. "No trouble is there? I can, can, can use
that eight bucks."

"No trouble," I said with a smile, leisurely returning wallet
and decoder badge to my pocket. "I'm just on a job that involves Mr. Lorre. In fact I had lunch with him a little earlier."

"Well, that's different, that's swell," said Eskian. "Right up those stairs, then to the right to the end of the hall and through the door with, with, with the photo of Betty Grable on it. Then up to the roof."

"Thanks," I said. "Oh, there's a guy out there on the street, looks a little like the big guy in Popeye cartoons."

"Bronko," said Eskian.

"Bluto," I corrected.

"Yeah," said Eskian squinting toward the street. "Right. I see, see, see him. What's he skulking around for?"

"He's with me. If he comes in, tell him I said he should wait, that I'd be down in a few minutes."

"Sure," said Eskian. "Always, always, always glad to help the police."

As I headed for the stairs in the corner, Eskian began to sing "The Night We Met in Honolulu."

His directions were fine, right down to the Betty Grable picture tacked to the door. The picture had been torn from a magazine cover. Betty was wearing a bathing suit and stood in profile looking back at the camera with a pouting smile. Someone had torn the picture in half and someone else had lovingly and not too expertly taped it back together.

I moved up the dark, narrow stairway, hearing voices above. I didn't count the steps but I figured it at about twenty. There was a thin open strip between the door and the floor of the roof at the top of the stairs. I groped for the door knob, found it, and stepped into the light.

A fat movie camera was set up in the center of the roof. It was an old camera on an old tripod and the camera operator was older than the camera, probably older than still photography. He wore a blue shirt and a frayed tweed jacket about twenty degrees too warm for the weather and his job. A kid who looked about twelve stood next to him holding a roll of tape. The kid looked over at me and picked his nose. Next to the kid sat a man in a metal folding chair. The man in the chair wore dark glasses and was an easy eighty years old. He wore a battered fedora and a pair of striped pants that didn't match his gray, patterned shirt. Beyond them, at the edge of the roof leaning against a waist-high brick wall, stood a man and a woman. The woman, at this distance, was pale, beautiful, with amazing red lips and hair as black as the Dragon Lady's. The man, a good four inches shorter than the woman, wore a suit and tie. His hair was combed straight back and glistened with pomade. He was a respectable double for Peter Lorre. I'll give him more credit than that. If I hadn't seen Lorre within the last two hours, there's a good chance I would have been fooled.

A portable radio sat on the pebbled rooftop next to the old man in the dark glasses. A female trio was singing, "Super Suds, Super Suds. Floods of suds for dishes and duds."

The old man in the dark glasses, who was facing me, suddenly shouted, "Radio off."

The kid stopped fooling with his nose and reached down to turn off the radio. Then he moved to a battered, black sound box on the ground and put on some old earphones.

"Better," said the old man in the glasses. "Now let's have a take here. Are you ready, Gregor?"

"I'm ready, Eric," replied the cameraman.

"Peter? Elisa?" shouted the man in glasses, who was still facing me with his back to the actors.

"Ready, Eric," the man and woman near the roof edge replied.

"Just say the right words, the ones in the script, and say them loud enough for me to hear even if we're not recording," the man in the chair shouted. "It will be easier to match it up later. No sticks, no anything. Gregor, roll the camera. Bobby, roll the sound."

"Rolling, Eric," said Gregor.

"Sound rolling, Mr. Steistel," shouted the kid with the earphones.

"Peter, Elisa. Act."

I leaned against the closed door and watched Peter and Elisa act. They argued. She turned her back on him. He cajoled in a fair imitation of Peter Lorre. She folded her arms. He spun her around angrily. She struggled. He strangled her and was about to throw her off the roof when the camera operator shouted, "Eric. That's the end of the scene."

"Then cut, cut, cut, cut," demanded Eric, slapping his thighs as he sat. "How did it look?"

"It'll do," Gregor said without enthusiasm.

"Fine," said Eric. "Let's set up for Peter's reaction shot. We've got to be back at the loft by four."

I stepped forward and began to head toward Sidney Kindem or Pete R. Lowry, who had lit a cigarette and offered one to Elisa, who accepted. I was even with the camera when the kid, who had taken off his earphones and picked up a roll of tape, stopped me.

"Hey, where you goin'? We're shooting a movie."

"Mr. Eskian sent me up," I said. "I've got to talk to Mr. Lorre."

"Who's there?" shouted the ancient man in the folding chair.

It was at that moment I realized that Eric, the director of this film, was blind.

"I don't know, Mr. Steistel," the kid said. "Some guy."

"Well, get him out of here, Robert," Steistel said, turning his head as if by some effort of sense or smell he'd pick up my location.

"I don't think I can, Mr. Steistel," the kid said, looking at me. "I'm an apprentice director."

"You are an apprentice everything," the cameraman named Gregor reminded him. "Help me move this camera."

"Intruder, who is the intruder?" shouted the blind director.

"Name's Peters," I said. "Toby Peters. I'm a detective." I started to reach for my Dick Tracy badge and realized I didn't need it.

"What are you detecting here?" he asked. "We've got a movie to make. A schedule to keep. Back in Germany we had a crew of people just to keep intruders like you away. And now . . ." he shrugged.

"Yeah," I agreed. "We all miss the good old days."

I bypassed the kid with the tape, moved past the camera, which Gregor was in the process of moving with great difficulty, and headed toward Kindem. He and the woman watched me advance with some curiosity. When I was a few feet from them, their curiosity had turned to mild concern. I don't seem to inspire warm feelings in people.

Elisa was not so young, not so beautiful up close. Her makeup covered a few lines she had probably earned. She didn't look bad but close-ups wouldn't be kind to her. Kindem looked even less like Lorre up close. He was heavier, taller. His eyes weren't as large and a layer of makeup helped cover pockmarks from a childhood bout with some pox. Some of the Lorre illusion came from the haircut, the way he held himself, and the makeup.

"Sid," I said. "I've got a question or two for you."

"For me?" Kindem said, opening his eyes wide, still in his act. The accent wasn't bad.

"Mildred Minck," I said.

"That's a question?" Kindem asked with a shrug, after taking a drag on his cigarette and looking at Elisa for support. She gave him none.

"I'm making it a question," I said. "I'm asking with a smile."

"Who," he asked, "is Mildred Minck?"

I took out Mildred's photograph and handed it to him. He examined it, squinted at it, held it at arm's length, shook his head and, taken altogether, did much more than he should have to show he was giving it a careful look and didn't recognize Mrs. Minck.

"I'm afraid I don't know this woman," he said softly, handing the photograph back to me. "Has she committed some crime?"

"She's missing," I said, holding the photo out to Elisa. Kindem started to reach out for an interception, but I held him off. Elisa took the photograph, looked at it, me, and Kindem, and returned it to me.

"Three years ago I was almost a star," she said.

"I remember," I said, but I didn't.

"Remember me in *Trail of the Lonesome Pine*?

"A small part, but you were beautiful," I said, looking at Kindem. "She really was. You've seen Mildred Minck? The woman in the photograph?"

"With him," Elisa said, pointing at Kindem with a well-polished fingernail.

"That is ridiculous," Kindem wailed, German accent no longer, soft whisper becoming shrill cry. "I have never . . ."

Elisa took a deep drag of her cigarette, threw the butt off the roof, let out smoke, and ignored Kindem.

"Cheap pictures with imitations," she said with what was supposed to be a withering glance at Kindem. "You know why this company is called Miracle Pictures? Because it's a miracle every time they finish a movie."

"That's not funny," Kindem said, returning to his Lorre character.

"I don't get paid enough to be funny," Elisa said.

"Ah," he said. "That explains it. You don't get paid enough to be funny or to act. You just mumble lines like a telephone operator."

"There's nothing wrong with telephone operators," Elisa said, leading me to the conclusion that she may well have been one not long ago, like yesterday.

"What's the use?" sighed Kindem, turning away from us.

"Where and when did you see Mildred Minck?" I asked Elisa.

"Yesterday, with him. Today, with him. I think they're planning a horror movie together."

"Ready for the next shot," Gregor, the old cameraman, said.

"Ready for the next shot," the kid with the tape repeated.

"Then shoot it," sighed Eric, the blind director, who seemed to have lost all interest in what was going on.

"I want to see Mildred Minck," I said sweetly to Sidney Kindem. "I will see Mildred Minck. I will see her today and you will tell me where she is or I'll rearrange your face so you can only do Marjorie Main and Wallace Beery imitations."

Kindem sneered but there was no heart in it. He would tell me where Mildred was and I could wrap all this up and go home to help Mrs. Plaut gather rubber for the war effort. I stepped back to watch as Gregor called, "Camera rolling."

The shot was a close-up of Kindem. We all got out of camera range and Eric called, "Shoot it," just as I heard the door to the roof bang open.

The shot was quick, sharp, and to my right. Everyone was to my right. Everyone plus Bluto and Mildred Minck, who were standing at the door. It looked like a badly posed publicity shot. Everyone stood around in horror. The gun, I couldn't tell what kind, had been thrown on the ground. Kindem, the imitator, had been shot. He crumpled, clutching his stomach, and looked as if he were going to plunge over the side of the building. I jumped past the rolling camera, jerked the dying actor back, and helped him lie down groaning.

"Death scene," he whispered. "God. I wish I could die like me. It's not right. A man should at least die as himself, you know what I mean?"

"Makes sense to me," I agreed. "Take it easy. We'll get an ambulance."

"That's a good idea," he said through clenched teeth. Then he said something in German I couldn't understand.

"An ambulance," someone called behind me.

"Who shot you?" I asked.

Kindem looked at me, bewildered, and then turned his head toward the others, who were all together except the kid who must have gone to call an ambulance. Kindem released his right hand from his bleeding stomach and raised a feeble finger toward them all.

"Which one?" I said. "A name."

"Steinholtz," he said, and he was dead.

"Steinholtz," I said aloud. "Did any of you hear him say Steinholtz?"

"I heard him," said Eric the blind director with irritation. "What is going on?"

Good. I had at least one other person who had heard Kindem identify the killer.

"Which of you is Steinholtz?" I asked, gently laying Kindem down on the roof. No one answered, but Bluto, who was standing next to Mildred, cried, "Get some help for him, for God's sake!"

"He's dead," I said. "Which of you is Steinholtz?"

"None of us is Steinholtz," Gregor the cameraman sighed. "My name is Steistel. Eric and I are brothers. The boy is Robert Parotti. I don't know those people." He nodded at Mildred and Bluto.

"Who is dead?" asked Eric the blind director.

"Lowry," said Gregor. "Someone shot him."

"Shot . . . shot our actor," he bleated, looking around with dead eyes for an answer or the killer.

"You," I said, looking at Bluto. "What's your name?"

Bluto couldn't take his eyes from the body. His mouth draped open. I'd been right about him in the Y gym.

"Your name," I repeated.

"Lebowitz. Michael Lebowitz," he said.

I'd heard the name before but I couldn't remember where, and then he supplied the answer.

"I'm Mildred's brother."

"OK," I said. "It figures. No one here is named Steinholtz. Let's try the other way. Did anyone see who shot him? Someone up here shot him."

"I didn't see a thing," said Eric despondently. "I haven't seen anything since August 13, 1927."

head," I said. "Would you like to save us all time and just confess? Would you like to say a little more to give the homicide cops an easy conviction?"

"I didn't shoot him," she said indignantly, brushing back the tower of dark hair that threatened to fall over her face. "I didn't have a gun. But I would have killed him if I had one."

A siren wailed. Paul Eskian wailed. Gregor Steistel began to pack his camera with an air of patient resignation while his brother sat with crossed legs and folded arms, brooding. Elisa lit another cigarette. Her hands were shaking but she delivered her line perfectly.

"I suppose this means the picture is off."

"No," said Eric. "The picture is not off. We get another Peter Lorre and we go on. We write something in. Years passing. Plastic surgery. A brother. Twins. Something. We might even have to pay a writer."

"Let's hope not," said Gregor.

"Someone should be sure he's dead," Mildred added. "And if he's not, someone should shoot him again."

"Mildred," I said as the siren approached the building and stopped, the squealing of brakes letting us know the ambulance had arrived, "Mildred, you should shut up."

"He's right, Mil," Bluto said, putting an arm around her which she shrugged off angrily. She was wearing a limp black dress and the look of a spoiled child who's been told she can't have the last peppermint stick.

"He lied to me," she said.

"He's probably very sorry about it," Elisa said. "I'm sure that if he were to be given another chance he would apologize."

Mildred shot Elisa a killing look.

"Are you ridiculing me?"

"But of course," Elisa shot back. "If you can't understand basic sarcasm, dear, I'll simply have to stop talking to or about you."

Michael restrained Mildred in the midst of her definite

"What happened on August 13, 1927?" Mildred asked.

"I would prefer not to discuss it," Eric said imperiously.

"And my name is Elisa Potter," Elisa said coolly. "Before my name was Elisa Potter, it was Elisa Morales."

"So," I said, walking past the camera, "no one is named Steinholtz and no one shot Kindem."

"His name was Lowry," corrected Eric.

"His name was Kindem," I corrected back. "I have a bad feeling in my gut that there won't be any fingerprints on that gun."

"Gun?" asked Eric, standing.

"About two feet in front of you," I supplied.

The door behind Mildred shot open and Bob, the boy assistant everything, and Paul Eskian ran in.

"What are you, you, you people doing up here?" Eskian moaned.

"Mostly dying," sighed Eric, reaching back to find his folding chair.

"You can't do this," Eskian moaned. "You were only supposed, supposed to shoot some stuff for a movie."

"We got carried away," Eric bellowed, turning his head to the sky. "The scene was going too slowly so I shot our actor."

"Hold it," I said. "I think everyone should be a little careful about what he or she says."

"Why?" said Eric with a laugh. "Are the police going to suspect me?" He held up his finger as if it were a gun and aimed it about five feet to my right. "I followed his voice, killed my actor, and threw the gun down knowing no one would see me."

"Well," I said with a shrug. "I've seen crazier things."

"I'd better go call off the ambulance and get the police," Bob said reasonably.

"Do that," I agreed.

"He deserved to die," screamed Mildred suddenly. "Deserved to die."

"I knew I could count on you, Mildred, to keep your

move toward Elisa, who didn't seem the least concerned. I figured it would be an interesting fight and I wasn't all that sure Mildred would be the favorite. I hadn't seen either of them throw a punch, a kick, or a snapping set of teeth, but Elisa's confidence reminded me of Max Baer in his prime.

A few seconds later two ambulance drivers in white came banging through the door, looked around, and headed for Eric.

"Not him," I said. "The one over there, the dead one."

The drivers, one compact and full of muscles, the other a pasty version of Victor Jory, stopped. The compact one was carrying a rolled up stretcher over his shoulder.

"Dead?" said the pasty one. "Why didn't someone let us know?"

"Sorry," I answered. "He died without warning."

"Look like a heart attack?" asked the compact one as the other guy went to kneel over the body.

"Yeah," said the pasty guy. "Something attacked his heart. Like a knife."

"Bullet," I corrected. "From that gun."

The two ambulance guys looked at the gun.

"Get it straight," the pasty one said with irritation. "This is a cop call, not an ambulance call. Next time be sure he's alive before you call us and if it's a shooting or knifing . . ."

"Or blunt instrument to the head," added the compact one.

"Or blunt instrument to the head," agreed the pasty guy, "or . . ."

"We don't need a catalogue," Elisa said.

"We'll call the coroner," Compact said, turning back for the door.

"Medical examiner," corrected Pasty.

"The police. Oh my, my, my God. The police," Paul Eskian wailed, looking at each of us for support, understanding. All this for a lousy eight dollars. Where was justice?

A new siren wailed toward us. This would be the cops. I didn't look. I kept my eye on the pistol to be sure no one made off with it or touched it. I walked over to it and knelt down to get a good look. It was a .38, not new, but in reasonably good shape. It had a slight scratch in the shape of an S on the barrel. A small triangular chip was missing from the wooden handle.

So, at least one question was answered. If this was the gun that had killed Sidney Kindem, I knew who it belonged to—a flat-nosed detective who would have a lot of explaining to do to the cops who were running up the stairs to the roof of Eskian's hardware store.

5

My brother is a cop. Did I mention that? Probably not. I try not to think about it but it keeps coming up, probably because we're in businesses that keep overlapping.

Phil is a captain in the Wilshire district. He's three years older than I am, overweight, nearing retirement. He has short, steel gray hair that he rubs with his right palm when he's at the last stages of trying to contain his rage and frustration, which was what he was doing now as I sat across from him in his office.

Phil would never have made captain if it weren't for the war. He didn't have the temperament for it. Actually, Phil had no temperament at all when he was playing cop. He had no sense of humor about crime. It made him angry. It wouldn't go away. I tried to tell him once that if there weren't any crime he would be out a job, that he should look at increases in murder, assault, and robbery as signs that business was booming.

He answered by saying that the job of real professionals was to eliminate their profession. Doctors were supposed to want to end illness. Dentists were supposed to want to end tooth decay.

"So, doctors, dentists, and cops have a suicide drive," I had said.

I wouldn't normally have said something like that to Phil but I'd just been arrested for obstructing justice and I was in a feisty mood.

I hadn't planned to obstruct justice this time or irk Phil even a little bit. I was getting too old for that. I'd been baiting my older brother for forty years. He'd been breaking pieces of me for the same time. I couldn't stop. Suicide drive. We both had it.

"How're Ruthie and the kids?"

That was it. Absolutely guaranteed to turn Phil Pevsner into Larry Talbot, the Wolfman. I never knew quite why my asking about his family did this. Maybe he thought it was some kind of dig at his being a provider. Maybe he thought I didn't see the family enough. Whatever it was, my asking about the Pevsner clan was high on the list of about two dozen things to say that could get my nose broken.

"They're fine," Phil said, playing with the empty coffee cup on his desk. "Lucy's got a cold or something, we don't know, but nothing bad. Dave's playing baseball and Nate's building stuff out of ice cream sticks. Ruthie . . . You know Ruthie. She just keeps going."

I didn't like this. When we were kids, Phil accepted only one night of truce, Thanksgiving. We stopped fighting long enough to break the turkey wishbone. I'd wish for a million bucks or a Tris Speaker glove. I didn't know what Phil wished for but I think it was chrome steel handcuffs.

King Kong was his favorite movie. I went with him to see it when it came out; he was just a sergeant in the L.A.P.D. His eyes went wide when Robert Armstrong as Carl Denham announced to the frightened crowd that they had nothing to fear, that Kong was chained with chrome steel.

"When we were kids, what did you wish for when we broke the wishbone on the Thanksgiving turkey?" I asked.

Phil was looking down at his desk. He gave a little chuckle and shook his head. Surely he would come after me now.

"Most of the time I wished I wouldn't have to grow up and work fourteen hours a day, six days a week in a grocery store like pop," he said. "Sometimes I wished mom wasn't dead."

"Phil," I tried. "I didn't kill that guy on the roof."

"I know it," Phil said, loosening his tie and looking up at me. Phil's eyes were gray, almost blue. He looked away toward the wall. This quiet resignation was worse than dodging Pevsner kicks.

"What the hell is going on here?" I asked. "What happened to my brother Phil? I don't know who the hell you are. You look like Phil. You sound like Phil. I can't think of why someone would want to do either one if they didn't have to, but whoever you are, you'd better come up with a good story or I'm calling a cop."

"They're retiring me, Tobias," he said. "Full pension. The works. I'll even get a medal."

"What are you talking about? You've got seven years to go till you have to retire. You didn't ask for an early retirement?"

"Nope," Phil said standing up. "They just don't know what to do with me. I haven't got the touch for this job. I rub people the wrong way."

He rubbed his right thumb along his fingers to show his touch. His hand looked calloused, a little hammy.

"I'm . . ." I started.

"They can't bust me back to lieutenant because they've got no charges and they can't use me downtown. Shit. I don't want to go downtown. I should have stayed on the street, Tobias. I'm a head-buster. I never liked making duty rosters and talking to ladies' clubs."

"Can't you . . ."

"No," he cut in. "I've got three months."

"I don't like you this way, Phil."

"I don't like me this way," he agreed. "Well, what the hell. It'll work out, right?"

"It'll work out," I agreed. "Now you mind getting me out of this?"

Phil stood up, stretched, and looked out the window. You could see the building next door or, if you bent down, a patch of sky. If you leaned right, you could see a narrow strip of

Wilshire. I let Phil look, sigh, and turn to the report on his desk. He picked it up, leafed through it, shook his head. "The crackpot people you get mixed up with, Toby."

"Phil, this is Los Angeles. That's the only kind there are."

"Blind movie directors, Peter Lorre imitators, runaway wives. It's a comedy."

"Better than a tragedy," I tried.

"Maybe so," he agreed. "No prints on the gun, not even yours."

"The killer wiped them off," I said.

"Why your gun? Why you? Where did they get it?"

"I don't know why, but I know where. The glove compartment of my car. That's where it was."

"Right where a car thief could get it and then maybe go out and shoot a few citizens," Phil said without anger. He was sounding more and more like a woeful, forgiving rabbi. I didn't need guilt. I needed my brother to push, drive me to look for answers.

"One of those people shot Kindem," I said.

"Which one, Steinholtz? Who the hell is Steinholtz? The only one with a motive was Mildred Minck, your client. The guy fooled her, got a chunk of dough from her, made her look like a stupid . . . I don't know what. She had motive. She knew your car. So did that brother of hers. They're the ones I should be holding, but I don't have evidence. None."

He sat down, folded his hands, and looked at me.

"Phil, you really think Mildred Minck or her brother shot that carbon copy?"

It was my turn to get up.

"No. I don't know," said Phil. "Maybe I don't even care. Get out. Go play detective. I've assigned Seidman to the case but he's up to his ass with other cases. He's got a hold-up team working around St. Vincent's, a wife who maybe did maybe didn't poison her husband with fertilizer, three other homicides. I've got more cases than . . . and all we've got around here are guys who should retire and 4-F kids. Ironic.

If it weren't for the damn war, I wouldn't have gotten promoted. Too many good-natured guys ahead of me. They all went into the army and I got a fast move up."

"We've been through that already. Can I go?" I asked leaning over the desk. "I can't stand to see an overgrown man cry and I don't like to hear the same complaint twice. I'm a suspect in a murder here. I have a right to some respect. Where's my grilling? What about the threats? No one's pushed me around, violated my rights. I'm getting the feeling I'm not wanted."

"You like, I'll turn you over to Cawelti," Phil said with a smile.

Sergeant John Cawelti was my ancient enemy. Cawelti looked like a Gay Nineties bartender with red hair parted down the middle and plastered down. His mustache flamed red with wax and he hated me with more than passion.

"Can I go?"

"Go," he said with a wave of his hand as he swiveled away from me on the chair and looked at the intriguing view of the wall across the way. "We're letting Mildred Minck go, too, at least until we come up with something more. Maybe we'll serve a warrant on that quack husband of hers for health code violations and hold her as an accessory. We're letting them all go."

"I'll see you, Phil," I said. I wanted to ask when I'd get my gun back but I knew better.

"Yeah," he answered, his back to me.

It was a little after five when I left the Wilshire station and took cab back to Beverly and Burlington to retrieve my car. The cabbie talked all the way about how some guy in a defense plant said women were doing better than men. Since the cabbie was a woman, I just grunted. Hell, maybe she was right. Maybe Phil should be replaced by Ruthie. Everyone liked Ruthie. I didn't think she'd clobber many bad guys, but she'd be great at the ladies' clubs. Somehow, though, I couldn't see skinny Ruthie in a uniform.

I gave the cabbie a nice tip for the short ride and wrote the amount in my notebook. Shelly was going to pay. I had found Mildred and, I guessed, she would be going back to him if he wanted her. I'd done my job, earned my day's wages.

The drive back to Mrs. Plaut's on Heliotrope was quiet. I listened to Tennessee Jed on the radio. "That a boy, Tennessee," said his faithful sidekick. "Got him. Dead center." Hell, maybe Tennessee Jed had killed Sidney Kindem.

I was tired, in need of a bath and shave and change of clothes. To escape the clutches of Mrs. Plaut was my greatest desire. I would gladly forgo finding out who killed Sidney Kindem if God would let me get past Mrs. Plaut, but God is a joker. If you want proof, just look in your local mirror.

"Mr. Peelers," she cried as I tiptoed up the stairs.

"Mrs. Plaut," I responded with a smile.

"I'm glad that you arrived early from whatever you do with bugs and things so that you can talk to Mr. Tortelli in re: his contributions to the scrap rubber drive."

She stood below me squinting through her glasses, hands on hips.

"I've had a trying day, Mrs. Plaut," I said. "I witnessed a murder, a murder with my gun. I've just been questioned by the police and I may lose my license."

"It sounds no different to me than your other days," she said. "A good night's rest and a worthwhile deed for country and hearth will make you feel like a new man. My mister used to say, work erases all doubt."

"He died of overwork, Mrs. Plaut," I reminded her.

"Perhaps," she conceded, "but he was in no doubt about who he was when the end came."

"A major consolation," I said.

"Mr. Tortelli," she said, waving at me with a thin, white finger and off to Mr. Tortelli's we went.

"Be persuasive, Mr. Peelers," she reminded me.

"I'll be persuasive," I said as we walked up the walk to the small, white house on the corner. The radio was on and Guy Lombardo was playing "East of the Sun." I knocked gently.

"No one's home," I said with a sad smile.

She pushed past me and hammered on the door.

"Coming, coming," called Mr. Tortelli.

Mrs. Plaut, not hearing radio or voice because she had chosen not to wear her hearing aid, pounded again.

"Coming, damn it," Tortelli cried, and appeared at the door holding a carrot.

He was a little man with a little belly who always wore suspenders. He had a little mustache and very little hair. Both mustache and hair looked like a bad dye job.

"What?" he asked looking at us. "I'm eating and listening."

"Mr. Peelers has a speech," Mrs. Plaut said, poking me in the side.

"Well, not exactly a speech, Mr. Tortelli," I said.

"Who're you?" Tortelli asked reasonably. "I think I seen you."

"I live in Mrs. Plaut's boarding house next door. My name's Peters." I held out my hand. He shifted the carrot to his left hand and shook my hand. "I don't believe in giving no rubber," Tortelli said. "That's before you start."

"Why?" I asked.

"On general principles," he said.

"Make your speech, Mr. Peelers," she urged.

"I pay my taxes," Tortelli went on. "I got a son in the navy, a daughter in the WACS. I buy defense stamps. You want to see my collection?"

"No thanks," I said. "But every piece of rubber helps."

"OK," he said.

"OK?"

"You convinced me," said Tortelli. "I got no time for this. I gotta get to work and I don't want you coming back. I'll go get something rubber."

I looked at Mrs. Plaut when Tortelli disappeared. She was smiling with approval.

"That was a good speech, Mr. Peelers," she said, patting me on the back.

"I didn't give my speech," I told her.

"Nonetheless," she said with sparkling triumph.

We stood on the porch listening to The Royal Canadians play and sing "The Lady in Red" and "All I Do the Whole Day Through" before Tortelli returned minus his carrot and plus a dirty automobile tire. He pushed open his screen door, deposited the tire in my arms, and slammed the door on us.

"I misjudged Mr. Tortelli," Mrs. Plaut said, taking my arm as we walked back down the street. My jacket, shirt, and pants were filthy from the tire I clutched in both arms.

"He's a saint," I said.

"Maybe we should bake him some raisin twinkle cookies," she mused.

"If anyone deserves them, it is Mr. Tortelli," I said. "Now where do you want this tire?"

I got the tire into Mrs. Plaut's garage and made my weary way back into the house and up the stairs. I stopped at the top of the stairs, got the L.A. telephone book, found a number, dropped a dime in the slot and asked the operator to get me the chief of police.

I didn't get the chief. I didn't expect to. I got a telephone operator who asked if she could help me.

"This is Deever Van Lewenhook," I said, pinching my nostrils. "I wish to speak to the chief of police."

"May I connect you with one of the chief's assistants, who will . . ." she began.

"This is Deever Houk Van Lewenhook," I repeated with a touch of pity at her ignorance. "President Roosevelt's deputy assistant for domestic interaction with urban law enforcement. I'm calling on behalf of the president of the United States and I really don't have much time. If you'd like to have your chief call me back at the White House in a few minutes, that will be acceptable but I can't really wait very long."

The trick was simple. The woman would never remember the name I'd given her, or the title. She might ask me again, if she had the nerve, but I'd make it even longer. It would be easier for her to put me through to the chief than risk screwing things up on a call back to the White House. She'd get on the phone to someone and tell him somebody from the White House wanted to talk to the chief fast.

"I'll connect you, sir," she said.

Seconds passed and a male voice came on.

"Can I help you?"

"Is this the chief of police?" I asked.

"No, sir. I'm his deputy, Deputy Chief Harkness and I'd be happy to . . ."

"Is there no end to this?" I said with weary patience. "Deputy Harkness, I have a long list of calls I must make for the president this evening. It is several hours later in Washington than it is in Los Angeles and I'm quite tired. If you'd like, I'll ask the president to get on the line right now and reassure you, but he is not in the best of moods. Mr. Molotov is due here within hours and . . ."

"OK, right, Mr . . ."

"Deever Houk Van Lewenhook," I said slowly and then, over my shoulder to an imaginary assistant, "Can you believe this? Don't these people read *The New York Times?*"

"I'll connect you with the chief, sir," Harkness said.

The chief came on a few seconds later. His voice was high and sounded as if it would soon crack.

"Mr. President?" he said.

"No," I sighed. "This is Deever Houk Van Lewenhook."

"I'm honored by your call," the chief said. "How can I help you?"

"One moment," I said and pretended to ask a question to someone behind me. I stuck the phone under my shirt and did a third-rate FDR imitation. "Tell him about Captain Pevsner and get on with it, Deever," I said. It was at that point I noticed Mrs. Plaut had come up the stairs and was watching me. I couldn't stop.

Into the phone I said, "The president asked me to tell you that a certain captain in the Los Angeles Police Department has rendered a most important service to the country, one which we are not at liberty to divulge till the war ends. It has come to the president's attention that this captain, Captain Philip Pevsner of the Wilshire District, will soon be retiring. We would like you to persuade Captain Pevsner to stay on the force, at least for the duration of the war. His services might again be needed. And please, do not let Captain Pevsner know that the president has intervened. It might even be best if you say nothing of this to members of your staff or the mayor."

"Captain Pevsner won't retire," the chief said. "Assure the president that I will persuade him to remain on duty."

"Fine," I said. "The president would like a brief word with you."

I looked at Mrs. Plaut, grinned, took my fingers from my nostrils, pushed my nose back and did my FDR.

"Chief," I said into the phone. "I wish to express not only my personal thanks for this service, but the appreciation of the entire country. In addition, I may well be calling on you to come to Washington for consultation on some matters of urban security, if you are interested in serving."

"I'd be honored, Mr. President," the chief said. This time his voice did crack.

Mrs. Plaut's mouth opened to speak and I hung up before her piercing voice could destroy the illusion.

"What are you doing, Mr. Peelers? Telephones are not for pranks."

"I was auditioning, Mrs. Plaut. Auditioning for a radio show. 'The Major Bowles Amateur Hour.'"

"You shall lose, I'm afraid," she said. "You'd best stick with editing and bug spray."

As she turned, the phone rang. Normally there was no beating Mrs. Plaut to the phone, but I was standing next to it and just managed to grasp it ahead of her.

"Plaut Boarding House," I said.

"Toby," came Phil's voice. "Get back down here."

"What's up?"

"A man named Imperatori got hit by a car on Rosabell near Union Station. He's dead. Another guy, a comic named Bernard, got a death threat on the phone."

"I got a feeling you're not just calling me to help clean up the morning blotter."

"Both guys are Peter Lorre imitators," Phil said.

"I'll be right there."

6

When I stepped into Phil's office, I knew things were back to seminormal.

"What kind of shit are you sitting in now, Toby?" he asked, collar open, coffee clutched in his right hand. His face was red and angry. He glanced down at a pile of reports on his desk.

Lieutenant Steve Seidman, Phil's former partner, a tall, pale man who always looked as if he knew how sad the world was and had a right to be, leaned against the wall holding his own cup. Seidman's tie was on. Phil's wasn't.

"Me?" I said innocently, looking to Seidman for sympathy and understanding. "I've got nothing . . ."

"We've got a witness says you were with Lorre this morning at Levy's Restaurant," Seidman said. "Less than two hours later a Lorre mimic gets shot with your gun."

"And now they're dropping all over the place," shouted Phil, smashing his cup down on the desk.

"Maybe the world will be a better, saner place without them," said Seidman, straight-faced, "but we can't go around using that for a reason or we'd have half the population of Los Angeles County on marble slabs."

"Toby," Phil said, looking at me as he leaned over with both hands on his desk, "talk to me."

"We talked this morning," I reminded him.

"That was before someone started collecting Lorre trophies," Phil said. "You know how many people in this town do Peter Lorre as part of some act or schtick?"

"Three hundred and thirty-seven," I guessed.

"No way of knowing," said Seidman, looking into his coffee cup sadly for an answer. "No way of knowing."

Since no one was going to ask me to sit, I pulled out the chair in front of the desk and sat.

"You might ask Lorre if he has some idea," I suggested.

"I saw him an hour ago," said Seidman. "Nothing."

Phil pounded the desk.

"Hey, you're not here to tell us how to run an investigation. You're here to answer questions. First, why did you go to see Lorre?"

"Shelly thought he'd run away with Mildred. I already told you that, Phil."

"Got it," said Seidman, who had put down his coffee cup and, still leaning against the wall, was taking notes.

"By tomorrow morning, this could be all over the newspapers, the radio," said Phil. "Some goddamn loony wants to get rid of Peter Lorre imitators."

"So do I," I said.

"But you don't, for Christ's sake, go around killing them," shouted Phil. "Or do you? Where were you all afternoon after you left here?"

"Collecting a rubber tire from Mr. Tortelli," I said. "That's T-O-R-T-E-L-L-I. It's for the scrap rubber drive. Mrs. Plaut was with me. That's P-L . . ."

"Knock it off," said Phil, coming around the desk toward me. "No jokes. Just answers."

I put up my hands to indicate that I would cooperate.

"OK." He went on pacing next to me, pounding his right fist into his left palm. "So Mildred Minck ran off with this fake Lorre."

"I went to the real thing first and found out it wasn't him," I explained. "Then I went to a theatrical agent I know to get a line on Lorre imitators. That led me to Kindem. He got shot . . ."

"With your gun," Phil reminded me.

"With my gun," I admitted. "And that was it."

"Lebowitz, Mildred's brother," Phil shot back.

"Maybe. Protecting his sister's honor, he shot the bastard who ruined her name," I said. "Makes sense. Lock him up. Case closed. Phil, I told you I didn't even talk to the guy." Which wasn't quite true.

A thick hand circled my neck and lifted me from the chair. I let out some kind of gurgle as Phil grunted, "I told you no jokes."

"Phil," Seidman said patiently, soothingly.

Phil dropped me back in the chair and I sat for a few seconds trying to reach the ache in my neck and ignore the dancing red amoebas I was seeing.

"On that roof," Phil said, walking back behind his desk to see if anything was left in his coffee cup (there wasn't), "What did you see?"

"I told—"

"Toby," Seidman cut in.

"OK," I sighed, and told it all again. "Now what?" I said when I'd finished.

"Now nothing," said Phil. "We work on it, hope this nut is finished, try to keep the papers from making a connection, go back to the suspects, find out where all of them were this afternoon. But it looks like our killer might not have been someone on the roof. Might have been someone who stuck his head in, shot, threw your gun down, and dashed to keep his next appointment in a busy day of Peter Lorre mayhem. Routine, Toby. Get out."

I didn't get out. Phil hadn't called me back to his office for this. He could have done everything but strangle me over the phone.

"That's it?" I said.

"It," he agreed sitting behind his desk and opening a file. "Oh, yeah, the chief of police just called. He's overruled my retirement. I'm staying on as captain right here at the Wilshire, at least through the war."

I looked at Seidman, who had closed his notebook and was giving me a wet-eyed warning look.

"Great," I said and got up. "When do I get my gun back?"

"Probably never. How's your neck?" Phil asked without looking up.

"I won't be playing mixed doubles for a few days," I said and got out of there in five steps and a slammed door.

I was halfway down the worn wooden steps just past the squad room that always smelled like pastrami and things I didn't like thinking about when Seidman caught up with me.

"He'd have been better off retiring," he said. "Blood pressure."

"Phil'd drop dead if he didn't have heads to smash," I said. "Don't you know the only thing between us and the jungle is Phil Pevsner?"

We moved over to let a uniformed cop drag a handcuffed, crying young man up the steps. The crying man needed two shaves and looked like a ragged nightmare.

"I've got a friend in the chief of police's office," Seidman said.

"Congratulations. I know a mechanic who can fix the automatic transmission on an Oldsmobile."

"Friend told a funny story a while ago," Seidman said, looking at me like a Jesuit urging confession. "I called him a while ago after Phil got his call from the chief. My friend said something about presidential phone calls. People with long names."

"Say Steve, I'd like to hear all this but I've got a neighborhood full of rubber shirkers to shake down," I said, resisting the urge to pat his arm.

Someone shrieked in the squad room. Neither of us seemed to notice. I would have bet it was the raggedy guy in handcuffs, but I hadn't seen the rest of the afternoon herd. I got out of there fast.

It was late, and I was hungry again. I drove back downtown and found a space on Hoover not far from the Farraday. Before going up to the office I stopped at Manny's Tacos on the corner. The dinner rush, all six of them, had departed. It was just me, Manny, and a woman with bleached hair, too much makeup and a too-ready laugh.

"What's the big fuss about Johnny Barrymore?" she asked as I sat at the counter and ordered two tacos and a Pepsi.

No one answered her so she asked again,

"The fuss, the big fuss. What is it anyway?"

"I don't know," Manny said, and I was sure he didn't.

"He's dead," I said. "Barrymore."

The woman laughed, a deep, rolling, false laugh. "A joker. God. Johnny was a joker too. He joked in bed too."

Manny shoved a plate with two tacos and refried beans in front of me. He plunked a bottle of Pepsi next to it.

"You want to know something about Johnny Barrymore?" the blond said, moving toward me.

I resisted the urge to lift my arm to protect my tacos. I didn't want to know anything more about John Barrymore. I wanted my .38 back. I wanted enough money to buy a new suit and stock my refrigerator and shelf. I wanted to eat my tacos in peace. I went for taco number one and took a bite so I wouldn't be expected to answer the blond's question. Manny had gone back to the end of the counter to lean against the wall with his arms folded while he smoked a Camel. He didn't want to know either, but it didn't stop the blond, who got closer and looked older.

She leaned forward to whisper to me, "Afraid he was going to get buried alive. That's a fact. Built it right into his will that they had to check it. Creepy, huh? Told me that right in bed one night, in the dark, when he was feeling vulnerable."

"That was in the paper," Manny said, apparently not afraid of offending a customer.

"I never," she replied haughtily, "never told the paper about me and Johnny. Never."

I ate my taco and planned my tactic for getting a few bucks

extra out of Shelly. The taco was fine, just greasy enough to remind me of trips to Mexico. And Pepsi never lets me down.

"He means about Barrymore being afraid of getting buried alive," I said between bites.

She walloped me soundly on the back and laughed while I choked.

"I don't read the papers," she said, glaring at Manny. "Right, my friend?"

"Lady doesn't read the papers, Manny," I said, getting my breath back.

"Forgive me for doubting you," said Manny sourly.

"Ha," said the blond, returning to her stool to brood.

I wolfed down my refried beans and washed down taco number two with a bravura finish of Pepsi. The I dropped sixty cents on the counter and left with a wave to Manny who deigned to do something that might have been nodding his head.

The Farraday lobby was empty, cool, familiar. It wasn't dark outside yet but the low sun was casting hard reds on the tile. I liked the way my footsteps echoed as I made for the stairs. I liked the feel of the black iron railing in my hand as I made my way up the stairs, ignoring the elevator.

There were still a few sounds in the Farraday, a machine rumbling, voices behind a door whispering, but there was nothing behind the door to the office of Sheldon Minck, D.D.S., and Toby Peters, Investigations. I used my key, though a hairpin would have done just as well. I groped for the light switch, hit it, and went for the door of the reception nook beyond which was Shelly's office, beyond which was my closet.

The bulb in the reception nook was a twenty-five-watter. Its light barely made it through the glass door with enough energy or interest to get me to the light switch inside. Shelly had pulled down the shades, probably to protect a burglar from the shock of seeing sanitary conditions the Red Cross wouldn't have tolerated in a prisoner of war camp.

"Don't turn on the light," a voice said after I'd walked across the room and reached up to the switch.

"I've seen it before, Shel. I can take it."

I turned to look in the room toward where Shelly's voice had come from. He was seated in the dental chair. Actually, he spent more time in the chair than all of his patients combined. It was his white swivel throne complete with a constant supply of running water.

"You joke. At a time like this, you joke," he said and I was sure he was shaking his head.

"I found Mildred," I said.

"I know. You think I don't know that? She came home."

"You owe me twenty bucks, closing fee," I said, flicking on the lights. "And you clean this place."

He was sitting in the chair wearing his wrinkled and stained smock. His eyes blinked; he looked like a startled, overfed mouse. His glasses were on his forehead, his dead cigar in his mouth. He reached up and flipped down the glasses and continued to blink in my general direction.

"She says it's all my fault, Toby. All my fault. She threw me out. Came home and threw me out."

He was pointing at himself through all this to be sure I knew who he was talking about.

"She ran away with a Peter Lorre imitator and it's your fault?"

I considered a cup of coffee to help suppress the tacos and refried beans that didn't want to be forgotten, but one look at the coallike demiliquid substance in the coffee pot made me give up Chase and Sanborn for the millennium.

"She says, Mildred says, I drove her to it. She says if I had been more attentive, she wouldn't have had to turn toward more glamorous men. She says if I hadn't sent you after her, Peter Lorre would be alive now."

"Shel, she didn't run away with Peter Lorre. Peter Lorre isn't dead. It was some fake."

Shelly blinked at me, removed the cigar, and put it back.

"She said . . ." he began.

"Mildred is distraught," I said.

"She says I had you go kill him," said Shelly, "but if it wasn't Peter Lorre . . ."

I couldn't see what difference it made in the long run who Mildred had run off with but I didn't want to explore it with Dr. Minck.

"Be that as it may," I began in my professional tone, "you owe me . . ."

"That's why he called. He wasn't dead," Shelly mused, bouncing his hairy, pudgy fingers together.

"Who wasn't dead, Sheldon?"

"Peter Lorre. Only I thought it wasn't Peter Lorre. You can understand. First he runs away with Mildred. Only you say he didn't. Then you shoot him. Which you say you didn't. Then he calls here and says he wants to talk to you."

"Which I will do," I said.

"He left a number somewhere," Shelly said with a pained wave of his arm.

"Where, Shel?"

"Who knows at a time like this, Toby. My world . . ." And he looked around at his world: The sink full of dishes and instruments sharing a shallow pool of water tinctured by coffee grounds, blood, and things too fierce to mention; a rusting green-enameled dental X-ray machine with a cone that looked like something Ming the Merciless had ordered for the express purpose of sadistically torturing Dale Arden; a glass-fronted cabinet of instruments crammed on top of each other and looking as if they yearned for freedom; a tall wooden cabinet filled with ancient dental books and browning dental magazines. Shelly's world was wondrous to behold.

"Shel, if Lorre hires me, you're off the hook for the twenty bucks."

"The number's Long Beach three four one two," he said without hesitation.

"Thanks," I said and went into my office. The shade on the only window in the room was up and there was enough sun to suit my need for light. Before I could get to the phone, I heard Shelly's radio playing through my closed door. Some band was playing "Poor Butterfly" and Shelly began singing along balefully.

I gave the operator the Long Beach number, sat through three rings, and got the same woman with an accent I had talked to earlier.

"Mr. Lorre, please. Tell him it's Toby Peters returning his call."

"Ah, yes," she said and put the phone down.

Somehow Shelly had gotten confused and was trying to sing the words to "Sleepytime Gal" to the tune of "Poor Butterfly."

"You'll learn to cook and to sew," he crooned. "What's more you'll love it I know . . ."

"Shelly, shut up," I shouted.

The hurt silence came immediately but the radio played on as Peter Lorre answered the phone.

"Mr. Peters?"

"Yes," I said.

"I seem to be in need of your services."

"What seems to be the problem?" I asked, considering a reasonable fee now that I knew he had a hefty Warner contract.

"This afternoon I mentioned that I might need your assistance. That was in reference to a threatening phone call. I get far fewer of those than you might think. In fact, this is the first since I left Europe. It might have been amusing if it were not for the fact he called again tonight and said that I was already dead twice and would soon be killed again. I'm dealing with a madman or a very humorless practical joker."

I asked the obvious. You have to ask the obvious or later you'll have to make up some lame excuse for why you didn't come up with something the average Cub Scout would ask.

"The police are . . ." I started.

"The police are an ass," he concluded. "I have informed them of this most distressing phone call and they have indicated the Los Angeles Police Department is unable to protect all the Peter Lorres in the city. I informed him that, to the best of my knowledge, I am the only Peter Lorre."

"And you want me to. . . ?"

"Serve as a . . . I don't know, a kind of bodyguard perhaps for a given period."

Someone behind him said something and Lorre excused himself politely, covered the mouthpiece, and then returned to me to say, "My wife indicates that I should pay whatever is essential."

"Twenty-five a day plus expenses," I said.

"That seems reasonable," he said.

"But I could be watching your back and front for weeks with you paying twenty-five a day. I don't object to earning twenty-five a day but there might be a better way."

"I'm all for improving our options," Lorre said.

"I put one of my men on you, watch you out of sight, and we find a safe place for you to stay for a few days while I go after whoever called you. If I find him, stop him in, say, a seven-day week, I get a one-hundred-buck bonus."

"That sounds most reasonable," said Lorre just as Shelly began to sing "Whispering" a cappella.

"Good," I said with a smile that most people took for pain. "You try to think of some place you can go for a few days. I'll come over there first thing in the morning and we'll talk about it. Just give me your address." He gave it and I went on, "I'll have one of my best men at your door before dawn. You won't see him but he'll be there. Man with plenty of experience, a good eye.''

Lorre said it would be fine but asked if we could meet in my office instead of at his home. He didn't want to disturb his wife. I countered with breakfast at Stan's on Sunset. He said he prefered Levy's. I suggested that it might be a good idea not to go to places he usually went to. He thought that might be a good idea. We said good-bye and I quickly added up my possible earnings. Two hundred and seventy-five bucks for a week's work, with one catch. I had to find a lunatic killer.

I had a few things going for me. Real crazies are not that hard to spot, especially around Hollywood, and they usually can't keep their mouths shut. If someone was going around hating Peter Lorre, he probably wasn't keeping it to himself. Probably. Unless he was keeping it to himself. On the other hand, I was on the roof when Sidney got shot with my gun and there were a limited number of suspects unless Phil was right and Kindem had only been one name on a checklist and the killer had shot him and run. But I had trouble buying that story, partly because of my gun and partly because I had a feeling that the dying man's Steinholtz was one of the people on that roof. I had to match Peter Lorre with someone on the roof.

Shelly was silent again as I pulled out my notebook and made a list of the suspects. The Steistel brothers, Eric the blind director and Gregor the dyspeptic cameraman; Bobby Parotti, the kid assistant; Michael Lebowitz, Mildred's brother; Mildred herself; Paul Eskian, the stammering hardware store owner; and Elisa Potter or Morales. There wasn't a good suspect in the bunch. Eric was probably eliminated, though I had seen stranger things than blind murderers. Back in '34, when I was still a cop, a guy had trained his monkey to shoot a gun. Worked with him every day for four months. Idea was the monkey would shoot the guy's wife and get away with it. The first time the guy gave the monkey a loaded gun, the very first time, the chimp or whatever it was shot the guy in the head. At least that's the way the wife told it. I always thought she was the one who trained the chimp and nothing had gone wrong at all.

OK. I had work to do. I went over the possibilities of people I could send to keep an eye on Lorre. Jack Ellis, the house detective at the Alhambra, used to back me up and give me an occasional fill-in night on weekends when the fleet was in, but Jack hadn't been the same since a pair of kid sailors had thrown him down the Alhambra elevator shaft. Jack wasn't all that enthusiastic about outside jobs any more. Paddy Whannel, a security guard at NBC, was getting a little gray for the work, but he was good, at least when he was sober, which wasn't often. Shelly was useless. Jeremy Butler might do it, but a bald 300-pound poet tends to be a bit conspicuous.

I picked up the phone and called Mrs. Plaut's. She didn't answer, proving that one's worst fears are not always realized. Mr. Hill the postman picked up the phone and I asked if Gunther were there.

"I'll check," he said and a few moments later Gunther's voice, precise, high, more than slightly accented, came on.

"That is you, Toby?"

"It's me, Gunther. I need a favor."

"Yes?"

"I need someone to keep an eye on my client, Peter Lorre. Someone may be trying to kill him. I want to be sure no one is tailing him when he comes to meet me for breakfast. If you could just watch him till tomorrow morning at about . . ."

"Where does he reside?" Gunther asked.

"I don't want to pull you away from your work," I said, even though that was pretty much what I wanted to do.

"A respite at this point would be most welcome. The project I am working on is a book on Soviet agriculture. My Russian is not as strong as it should be and my knowledge of agriculture minimal."

"Sorry I can't give you a hand," I said.

I gave Gunther the address. I didn't have to describe the client. When we hung up, I tried not to think of what a three-foot-tall midget could do if Lorre were attacked, but Gunther had done pretty well in the past. I tried not to think of how conspicuous a three-foot-tall midget might be tailing a man, but decided that a little man would hide more easily than a giant or a fat, myopic dentist. Besides, he could stay in his car, and all he had to do was watch Lorre's rear end.

A knock at my door pulled me from sweet reason to Shelly's face. The door opened before I could tell him to come in.

"I'm busy, Shel," I said.

"I'll wait," Shelly said with a smile, a large bead of perspiration wending its way down his forehead.

"I may be all night," I said with a smile as large as his.

"That's what I wanted to talk to you about, Toby. How long have we been friends?"

"I wouldn't say we're exactly friends, Sheldon," I said, still smiling. "But, to give it the benefit, five, maybe six years."

"Five or six years," he repeated, shaking his head. "Time really flies."

"Shel . . ."

"I need a place to sleep tonight."

"Hotel," I said, looking down at my list of suspects.

"Mildred didn't let me stop for the money in the Buddha. I'm broke. Just one night, Toby. I'll sleep on the floor."

I think he was about to go down on one knee and beg. I'm not sure. But I didn't give him the chance.

"One night?" I asked. "And I'll sleep on the floor. I always sleep on the floor."

"One night, and then I'll get to the bank. I've got two hundred in the bank. First thing in the morning. Cross my heart," he said, wiping his forehead with his dingy sleeve. "We roomed together in New York. I wasn't so bad."

"One night," I agreed with a sigh. "I'll be ready in about ten minutes."

"Toby . . ."

"If you say 'God bless you,' the offer is off."

He put his fingers to his lips and slipped out the door, closing it behind him. He sang no more while I put my notes together and settled on a plan for the morning. When I stepped into his office, Shelly stood holding a dental case in his right hand.

"Got some homework to do, Sheldon?" I asked.

Shelly looked down at his bag and held it up in front of him as if I could see through it.

"Change of underwear," he explained. "Managed to grab it when Mildred turned her head."

"I'm grateful," I said. "Let's go."

And we did. But we didn't get far. Outside the door of our offices, on the floor of the hallway of the Farraday Building, lay a dead pigeon with a little capsule tied to his leg.

"How did a bird get in here?" Shelly asked, holding his case under his arm and moving to kick it out of the way.

"Hold it, Shel," I said, and leaned down to pop off the top of the capsule and pull out a rolled up note.

"What's it say?" Shelly asked, pushing his slipping glasses back on his nose. "Who's it for?"

7

Around midnight Shelly called my name. I opened my eyes and looked up from my mattress on the floor at a cool finger of moonlight touching my small kitchen table. I pretended not to hear him as I rolled over on my side, closing my eyes.

"Toby," he repeated, "I don't get it. Who would kill a pigeon? Who did a pigeon hurt? I'm not going to be able to sleep."

I considered a convincing snore, rejected a grunt that he might take for attention, and discarded the idea of telling him I wanted to get some sleep. I am not without sympathy for murdered pigeons but Shelly seemed to have missed the point. Inside the capsule attached to the pigeon's leg was a simple message to me: PETERS FORGET THE LOWRY MURDER OR YOU ARE A DEAD PIGEON.

"Toby, you awake or what? I can't sleep. Let's play gin or talk or something."

I didn't want to hear about Mildred. I didn't want to hear about a new scheme for wiring teeth so you could pick up radio stations in your mouth. I wanted to sleep. I had a big day ahead of me and I wanted to dream about Puffed Rice covered with five spoons of sugar and milk to the top of the bowl.

Shelly gave up after a few more mild whines and whimpers and I slept. If I had been alone, I would have gotten up for the cereal, but it wasn't worth the price I'd have to pay in conversation with Sheldon Minck.

I dreamt. Jeremy tells me that we all dream every night but we don't remember our dreams. The trick to remembering is to wake up during a dream. Poets, he said, are particularly good at waking up during or immediately after a dream. Something lets them know some good stuff that they might be able to use has been going on. Jeremy's current favorite poet was Byron. I read a few Byron poems. The guy had nightmares. I preferred the book of William Blake poems Jeremy had given me, though I didn't understand most of them. I just liked the way they sounded and it was the only poetry book I'd ever seen with drawings in it.

I dreamt. It was a dream I thought I was rid of. Cincinnati again, I thought as I dreamt. I wandered the streets, went down to the water. There was a dead pigeon floating in the river. I didn't take a good look at his face. I kept walking. The damned city was empty, as empty as it always was. This time it wasn't winter. It was summer and the only sound was a flag on a pole high above me flapping in the wind. I went wandering, knowing I wouldn't find anyone. I never did. There were different places in Cincinnati where I usually wound up. One place was on the shore of the river looking out at an island. Another place was a row of old townhouses. I didn't want to go there but that was where I found myself. I went up the stairs of one of the identical townhouses, closed the door behind me, listened for nothing, and heard a knock at the door. I turned in fear and started to reach for the door handle and then I stopped just as I always stopped. I didn't want to see who or what was out there. I had wandered around Cincinnati, where I've never been, looking for life, for something, and now that it was right outside the door, the possibility of facing it panicked me.

I woke up suddenly, choking back a shout. Morning light came through the window. I was sweating. Shelly was snoring gently in the bed. I remembered the dream but I didn't play with it. I wanted it to go away. I got up carefully, paying tribute in caution to my back. Nothing hurt. I took off my T-shirt, threw it on the sofa, and looked at Shelly, who resembled a beached seal on its back.

Sitting at the table, I ate my Puffed Rice with slices of my last banana after eating the cream from the top of the new bottle of milk with a reasonably clean spoon. I felt better.

"Mildred?" Shelly called out, sitting up and looking in my general direction with a nearly closed-eye squint. His chubby body quivered in something that might have been hope.

"No, Shel," I said. "It's me."

He reached over to the table near the bed, groped for his glasses, found them, pushed them on his face, and found me.

"Toby," he said. "I thought . . ."

"Want some cereal?"

He waddled over in his drooping shorts and we ate in near silence, except for the sounds of a despondent dentist playing with his breakfast. His cereal got soggy. I got up and put together enough clothing to make myself almost presentable if someone didn't look too closely at the shirt, which was missing a single button right in the middle. I covered that missing button by wearing my poplin jacket zipped closed. No one could see the holes in socks, shorts, or ego.

"How do I look, Shel?"

He shrugged and popped a grain of Puffed Rice on the table with the back of his spoon. I checked the small mirror on my dresser near the Beech-Nut clock, which told me it was 8:30.

"I need a shave," I said.

Shelly said nothing.

"I'm going to shave, Shel. You might make the bed, get dressed, and make your way to the bank so you can stay somewhere else tonight."

"Whatever," Shelly said, reaching into the cereal box to find another cereal morsel to crush.

I grabbed my razor and went into the hall humming the Gillette Blue Blade song.

"How are you fixed for blades?" I crooned.

And a voice inside answered, "There are no blades in Cincinnati."

It scared the hell out of me, made me consider religion or something stronger than the couple of beers a week I usually put away. I knew no one was there but me, but I didn't like what I was doing to myself.

"Comes from being alone so much," Mrs. Plaut's voice said from the stairwell.

"What does?" I asked.

"That look, talking-to-yourself look. I see it in the mirror once or twice a day," she said, taking the last few steps up the stairs to the landing and pointing her broom at me. She was wearing her hearing aid this morning. "Doesn't scare me anymore, though."

"Doesn't?" I said.

She shook her head.

"You get used," she said.

"Used?"

"Used to it," she said. "You never like it, but you get used."

"You've made me feel much better, Mrs. Plaut," I said with a tip of my razor in her direction as she approached the door to my room. "Maybe I'll just go in there and cut my throat."

"Won't," she said with a hand on my doorknob. "You're not a croppler."

I wanted to warn her about Shelly sitting in my room in his shorts. He was probably croppling, whatever that was. I went in the bathroom and shaved.

A few minutes later I finished shaving and stuck my head in my room, where Mrs. Plaut sat at the table across from Shelly saying, ". . . and when I let my mister come back he was as well-behaved as Teddy Roosevelt's dog."

I reached over, put my razor on the dresser, closed the door quietly, and tiptoed down the stairs. It could have been a good day. The sun was out, the sky blue and clear. Halfway down the block some kids I couldn't see were laughing on their way to school. My back was feeling fine and I had a few dollars in my battered but still serviceable wallet.

It could have been a good morning or, at worst, a passable one if someone hadn't chosen that moment to take a shot at me. I recognized the sound, the whistle of a miniature super-speed train buzzing past, and the crack of glass behind me. It was the crack that convinced me I wasn't hit, or probably wasn't hit. The shot could have gone through me. But I've been shot twice and it wasn't like this.

I dropped and kissed Mrs. Plaut's white-painted porch and waited for the second shot. None came. A car screeched away, wasting precious tire rubber that could have been used by FDR for the boys overseas.

People didn't come running out of their houses. The kids on their way to school kept laughing and the sun kept shining. I wondered how long I would writhe there if the bullet had pinched its way through me.

Sitting up carefully, I double-checked to be sure there were no holes in me. I turned my head and saw that there was a distinct hole in the photograph of Eleanor Roosevelt that Mrs. Plaut proudly displayed in the belief that it was Marie Dressler. Eleanor wore the bullet hole like a pendant as she stared in the general direction of the departed gunman or -woman through cracked picture glass.

I could have yelled, moaned, looked around for sympathy, called the cops, but I knew that no matter how much the incident had meant to me it wouldn't register on other people as more than an annoyance, a call for attention and sympathy. I brushed myself off and walked down the steps, watching both ways for returning assassins. I didn't let myself get truly scared till I squeezed into my Crosley. My body was scared, but my mind didn't seem to be. My hands shook and I felt cold, but I felt myself waiting for my body to get over it so I could get on with business. After all, my mind told my body, maybe it was a mistake. Maybe the would-be killer was a Republican and was going around shooting framed photos of the Roosevelts on his way to work. Or perhaps he was after someone else, a neighbor, or even Mrs. Plaut, who had made many inadvertent enemies at the War Ration Board. I drove and tried to calm my body with other possibilities, but my body just kept shaking and insisting that it knew it had been the target. The most likely gunman was the one who had left the message with the pigeon, but hell, he wasn't playing fair. He hadn't even given me a chance to get out of the case before he came shooting. Then again, this could simply have been a second warning.

I turned on the radio and it helped. The Blue Network news was reporting that German vengeance squads had wiped out Lidice, a Czech village of about 1,200 people, killing all the men and deporting the women and children on the grounds that the people of the town were harboring the two assassins of Reinhard Heydrich, the hangman, the late German ruler of Bohemia-Moravia. A guy taking a shot at a middle-aged detective on a Hollywood street didn't seem very important, even if I was the target. Instead of wondering about my shootist, I wondered where Lidice was. I realized that I wasn't even sure where Czechoslovakia was. I was pretty sure the Czechs hadn't invited Heydrich to be the ruler of Bohemia-Moravia.

The radio went on to say something about the exiled king of Greece visiting the White House but my heart wasn't in it. My heart was somewhere near my frayed black belt.

The restaurant was just off San Vincente. It had a lot to recommend it. There were always parking spaces nearby and very few people died of food poisoning as a result of eating at Stan's. I knew Lorre was already inside because I spotted Gunther's car halfway down the block with Gunther's eyes peering just over the steering wheel in the direction of the restaurant. I parked and walked over to Gunther, who rolled down the window.

"He's inside," I said.

"He is inside," Gunther confirmed. "He came directly here from his home. No one followed."

Gunther had been up all night watching Lorre's house but you wouldn't know it to look at him. Twenty out of twenty passing strangers asked to judge which of us had been up all night would have chosen me without hesitating. Gunther's face was clean shaven, his hair neatly combed. As always he wore a three-piece suit that didn't display a wrinkle. I couldn't see his shoes but I was sure I'd be able to see my reflection in them if he got out.

"I'll take over now, Gunther, thanks."

"It would be no great inconvenience for me to continue the vigil," he said. I thought I heard a background strain of tiredness.

"No, I'll call you later if I need relief. I'll find a place to keep him safe till I can figure out what's what and who's who."

"What's what and who's who? An idiom?"

"You got it, Gunther," I said, looking over at the restaurant and down the street in case I had been followed by my sniper. I had not ignored the possibility that the guy who had taken a shot at me had also killed two Lorre impersonators, one with my gun.

"Then I shall depart, Toby. Please exercise caution."

"At all times," I said with a grin.

Gunther didn't believe it, but he turned on the ignition, put his feet on the built-up gas and clutch pedals, and eased out into the street.

Lorre was sitting at a window table near the front of the restaurant with his back to the door. The place wasn't crowded but there were a few late breakfasters and four old guys arguing at a table in the back. I walked over to Lorre and said, "Good morning. Let's change tables."

"But," he said, looking up from a plate of something with eggs, "the day is . . ."

"You don't sit near windows and you don't turn your back on doors," I explained. "Not till this is over."

"I see," he said through hooded eyes. "Then you think. . . ?"

"When I can," I said. "But mostly I know from having done it wrong too many times."

Lorre got up, took his napkin and silverware in one hand and his plate in the other, and followed me to a semidark windowless booth away from the front of the restaurant.

"Where you goin'?" asked a waitress behind us.

"Booth," I explained, turning to her.

"I've been on my feet since five," she said.

She was a good forty pounds overweight. I felt sorry for her feet. I said so and watched Lorre sit down in the booth and arrange his breakfast. Then I sat across from him where I could watch the door.

"Now I've got to walk another ten, fifteen feet," she said, standing over me with her pad. "You count coming and going, you add on a half mile a day for every table past station six."

"Would you like eggs Benedict?" Lorre asked, nodding at the stuff in front of him. "I must confess I am partial to dishes that seem even a bit more exotic than the usual fare. It comes from sleeping on park benches in Vienna when I was a young man, when I was locked out of the house by my stepmother for not getting home before nine. I stayed away from home for weeks. I sold my books, my clothes for food, and when I had no more books or clothes I lived on coffee and conversation and watched others eat."

"I'll try the eggs Benedict," I said, and Lorre nodded at the waitress.

"Coffee?" she asked, shaking her head, unable to get over the death march we had imposed on her.

"If we don't sit back here," I explained, "somebody may come in and shoot us before we can see them."

"Coffee?" she repeated.

"Coffee," I said, and she limped away.

"Someone shot at me this morning," I said, reaching for a piece of cold toast.

Lorre had a piece of running egg near his mouth, but stopped before he could get it in. He couldn't decide whether to eat it or put it back. He ate it. I liked that.

"And you believe . . ."

". . . in being careful," I said. "I don't know what's going on. We can go through a list of possible enemies or I can put pressure on everyone who was present when the first guy got shot on the roof."

"Which would you prefer?" he asked.

"They used my gun on the roof," I said, crunching the end of the toast and cursing myself for not seeing the small jar of red jam in the shadows of the napkin holder.

"I see. That offends you?"

"No, it makes me think someone knew which car was mine. I had the gun in my glove compartment. It makes me wonder why they picked my gun, why they were following me. It makes me think one of the people on that roof pulled the trigger. Maybe there's a club of Peter Lorre haters in Los Angeles. Maybe the shooting on the roof had nothing to do with the other killing and the phone threat to you. It could all be coincidence, a sudden epidemic of Lorre hatred."

"It is unlikely," Lorre said, calmly downing the last forkful of food on his plate. "But it could have something to do with hatred of Germans. I've played Nazis even though I fled from them. Who else is playing Nazis but Jews like me who ran from Europe with whatever we could carry. My grandfather was a rabbi. My real name, which I can hardly remember, is Ladislav Lowenstein. Yet I've had hate mail asking why a Nazi like me was getting rich making American movies. Perhaps . . ."

"I don't think it's a Nazi hater. No one's taking shots at Conrad Veidt or trying to run down Otto Preminger or Fritz Lang—at least I don't think they are," I said as the waitress plopped the plate and cup of coffee in front of me.

"But they are not as visible as I am," Lorre countered.

"Might be a little cold," the waitress said, sponging up some spilled coffee with a paper napkin. "Had to carry it further."

"I'm sure it will be lovely," I said, showing a false smile and lots of teeth. She turned and moved away.

"I think that woman is indifferent to the possibility of obtaining a tip," Lorre said, lighting a cigarette.

"Maybe," I said, "but I like her."

Lorre laughed and said, "You are most amusing, Mr. Peters, most amusing."

"You said that in some movie," I said, cutting into the eggs Benedict.

"I've said practically everything in some movie," he said with a shrug. "Everything but obscenities and perhaps I'll live long enough to do that also."

Eggs Benedict wasn't bad at all. It wasn't even cold.

"Good stuff," I said.

"You have a plan?" he asked.

"I have a plan," I answered and I told him the plan. Part one of the plan, as I'd told him on the phone, called for him to get out of his house with his wife and stay somewhere for a few days, somewhere where he couldn't be found. I'd watch the front door and he could go out the back. Part two called for him to return for a meeting I wanted to hold of Peter Lorre imitators. We could both warn them, which appealed to Lorre, and maybe find some reason for the murders. We might also lure the killer into the open.

"And how do you propose to get these people together?" Lorre asked reasonably, sipping his coffee.

"We spread the word that we're auditioning people who can imitate you for a movie. I know just the movie."

"Excellent, but might this not also draw the killer to . . . ah, I see," he said putting his finger to the side of his nose.

"You got it," I confirmed. "We can't watch you and every mimic in Los Angeles, but if we get them all together and draw our killer, we can . . ."

". . . get someone killed," Lorre finished.

"Or save someone," I said as the waitress roamed over with the check, looked at each of us and decided that the actor was a better choice to pay the tab.

"Yes, I suppose so," agreed Lorre as the waitress hovered over us.

"Carol's on break," she said. "You can pay me."

Lorre put his cigarette in his mouth, reached back for his wallet, and came out with a five-dollar bill, which he handed to the woman. She examined the bill suspiciously and moved slowly off to get his change.

"And when shall this scene take place?" he asked, placing his wallet on the table.

"Tomorrow. It'll take that long to get the word out, find a place to get everyone together, get backup people to cover the place."

"I see," said Lorre, looking at his wallet. "And that will cost. . . ?"

"Give me a hundred and hope for change."

"Check?"

"Perfect. You think of a place to stay for a few days?"

"The old man has a little place in Santa Monica. I'll move into it till tomorrow," Lorre said, pulling out a checkbook and opening it to a blank page. "I'm between pictures at the moment."

"Your father's here?"

"My father? I see. No, Sidney Greenstreet's the old man. He's quite willing to help out. I've already called him."

Lorre gave me Greenstreet's address and the telephone number in Santa Monica. We left after I checked the street, grinned at the waitress, and grabbed a mint from the cashier's counter. An hour later Lorre was packed and out of his home with me checking the street and assuring myself that no one was on his tail or mine.

Lorre drove himself to Santa Monica and I headed back downtown, going up Broadway, through Elysian Park, and down Gatewood Street. Half a block from the Los Angeles River on Gatewood I found the house I was looking for and parked in front of it. The front door of the house was open and Bing Crosby was singing "Mississippi Mud" from a radio or record player inside.

8

The house was a small white frame box with the paint peal-
ing off. It sat between two almost identical frame houses
whose paint was peeling even faster. All three houses looked
as if they were floating on a small lake. A fire hydrant had
broken and was lazily bubbling mud around the three dwell-
ings and threatening to spread to a run-down adobe down the
block.

I was trying to figure out how to get to the house without
ruining my only pair of shoes when she stepped out on the
porch.

"I just called the fire department," she said. "They'll come
out and turn off the hydrant. Kids keep doing it."

She was wearing a white apron over a yellow dress and her
hair was tied back with a yellow ribbon. She looked like the
full-page ad for a Glo Coat floor in *Collier's*.

"I'm looking for Elisa Potter," I said.

"You found her, Peters," she said in a voice I knew, attached to a face I didn't. "But at home I'm Elisa Morales."

The face was almost free of makeup and as she stood there
looking at me with her hands on her hips I had the eerie feeling that she was my wife and I was coming home from work
to one of the problems homeowners dread and have to face a
dozen times a year.

"Why don't you take off your shoes and socks, roll up your
pants, and wade over?"

I sat on my fender, removed my shoes and socks, tucked

them under my arm, and took her advice. The muddy grass
sucked at my feet and I felt my left pants leg start to fall so I
leaped forward to the porch to save it from a cleaning bill as
Bing crooned, "It's a treat to beat your feet on the Mississippi
mud."

Elisa was leaning on the porch rail and regarding me with
amusement.

"You looked like a crippled stork," she said.

"Thanks. I was doing my best to impress you. Glad it
worked."

I put the shoes and socks on the porch and shook as much
mud and moisture from my feet as I could.

"You like tamale pie?" she asked, folding her arms and
stepping toward me.

I could smell something minty on her breath.

"Love it," I said, which was the truth.

"Hungry?"

"As usual," I answered, following her toward the screen
door.

She turned, held out her hand, and said, "Wait. I'll get you
some water and a towel for your feet."

She went in and I waited. Bing stopped singing and the
sound of a needle scratching in the final rut let me know it
was a record and not the radio. A plop let me know that the
next disk had dropped and the Andrews Sisters confirmed it
by belting out "Hold Tight." The screen door pushed open
and a small wet towel sloshed toward me. I caught it, cleaned
the mud off my feet, dried them on the straw welcome mat
and put my shoes next to each other on the mat with my socks
inside them before going inside. I followed the smell of chili
powder and pepper through the neat but not expensively fur-
nished living room and passed through a doorless arch into
the kitchen.

Elisa, pot holders in both hands, was placing a big iron pot
on a smooth stone in the middle of the table.

"Have a seat," she said, nodding toward a wooden chair. I sat.

She went to the cupboard, got a couple of bowls and forks, and came back to the table.

"Smells great," I said.

"Tastes great," she said, clearing a spot for herself with her hand by pushing away garlic husks and remnants of celery. "My mother was Mexican. From Juarez. Her people have been making tamale pie from before Cortez. Beer?"

"Sure," I said, and she went to the refrigerator, pulled out two bottles of Meister Brau beer, pulled off the caps with a bottle opener attached to the refrigerator, and returned to the table.

"Serve yourself," she said. "I was hoping someone would come by. Thought I'd have to give some to the Larkins next door. Rita's all right, but Charlie can't keep his hands in his pockets and off the hostess."

She served me a full bowl and a huge chunk of rough wheat bread.

"Will you marry me?" I asked.

"No thanks," she said. "I tried it a couple of times. Didn't like it."

We ate in silence, listening to Crosby, Patti, Maxine, and Laverne, and Dinah Shore records. Neither of us said a word till we'd finished and had a second beer.

"Great," I said. "Thank your mother for me when you see her."

"Mom's dead," she said, starting to clear the table.

"Sorry," I said.

"She was ninety-two," said Elisa with a smile. "She had me when she was almost sixty."

"Some woman," I said.

"I've got a younger brother," she countered, stacking the final dishes in the sink and wiping her hands on the apron. I sat looking at the bottle of Meister Brau as she took off the apron, found her purse and a pack of Camels, and lit up after sitting across from me.

"I didn't kill him," she said.

"OK," I said, taking in a gulp of beer.

"I hardly knew Sidney," she went on.

"Fine," I said.

"I mean, I can be tough enough on the set. You have to be. And I can't say I liked the twerp, but I didn't shoot him. Why would I?"

"I can't think of a reason," I said. "I'll be happy to cross you off my list as soon as you answer a few questions. But you've got to admit that I wouldn't be much of a detective if I crossed everyone off a suspect list just because they told me they didn't do it and let me sit barefoot in their kitchen eating tamale pie."

"Why would I kill Sidney Kindem?" she asked again.

"Because he looked like Peter Lorre?" I asked in return.

"What?"

I wasn't getting very far with this, but I wasn't really interested in going on. I had a pleasant attack of heartburn and a couple of beers in my stomach. I was going through the motions.

"Someone's been going after Peter Lorre imitators since Sidney took a bullet yesterday," I explained. "Sidney was the first, or maybe not if there's a body or two waiting to be found."

"Coffee?" she asked.

"Sure," I said and watched her get up, go to the pot, get the cups, and come back.

"You'd make a great wife," I said, smelling the coffee. "Hills Brothers?"

"Yeah," she laughed, pouring herself a cup. "You'd think so. But I lost the role. Got the wrong leading man twice. You know something, Peters?"

"Toby," I said.

"Toby," she repeated. I liked the way it sounded. "You know something, Toby? I'm not much of an actress. I can deliver a line if it doesn't require too much feeling, and I'm fine in medium and long shots. I move all right . . ."

"You move more than all right."

"I move all right but I don't have whatever it is that comes across in a movie," she said, not quite ignoring my comment. "So I do low-budget quickies and make a living. Sometimes I go down to Mexico and do a picture in Spanish for a few dollars. I'm saving to buy a restaurant, a good Mexican restaurant where I can sit in a hot kitchen, cook tamale pie, and get fat like the rest of my family. The hardest part of acting for me is staying thin. It's unnatural."

"You look fine," I said, leaning toward her.

"You're fun," she said, leaning close enough to me so I could smell the mint on her breath again, the mint and chili.

She smiled and cocked her head and then the smile left her. She looked over my left shoulder toward the doorway to the living room. I turned and found myself looking at a dark, handsome young man with muscles and yellow anger in his eyes.

Elisa said something in Spanish to the young man.

The young man said something angrily to Elisa and advanced on her with closed fists. She got up to face him and kept talking in Spanish. I tried finishing my coffee but the young man hit my shoulder, spilling what was left on the table.

Elisa screamed at the young man, who grabbed her right arm. She slapped at his hand and pulled away. It was time. I got up, took a step, and put myself between them. His perfectly white teeth were clenched in front of my face.

"Excuse me," I said. "If you're going to speak Spanish, you'll have to slow down a hell of a lot for me to understand you. And if you want to push the lady around, you're going to have to go around me to do it and I'm not so easy to get around."

"Out of the way old man," the kid snarled. "I don't want to have to hurt you."

"That's all right," I said through my crooked grin, "I fight dirty."

His knee came up fast to let me know that kids could fight dirty too, but he telegraphed that it was coming by shifting his weight and biting his lower lip. He would have made a lousy boxer in spite of the perfect build and body. Everything showed on his face. I turned my hip into the knee, threw my right elbow into his stomach, and hit him with an open-handed short left to the jaw that shot him backward over the chair I'd been sitting in.

Behind me Elisa shouted, "Stop!"

The kid came rolling up from the floor and came off his knees with a knife he'd grabbed off the table.

"Hold it," I said. "Before someone really gets hurt."

The someone I was most concerned with was me, but I had taken on some responsibility for Elisa and I held in a mad urge to make a barefooted dash past the kid for the front door. He came at me, knife low, blood on his teeth.

"Ernesto," Elisa cried behind me.

I took three quick steps toward the living room to Ernesto's right and he lunged after me, but I stopped, leaned left and kicked up with my right foot. My toes hit his already pummeled stomach and Ernesto went down, the knife flying and in a one-in-a-million chance plunging into a photograph of a toothless old woman on the wall.

Ernesto rolled in pain on the floor and I turned to Elisa to ask her if she was all right. The answer was the metal bowl of a soup ladle against my right cheek.

"Mama," Ernesto groaned from the floor.

The groan saved me from a second crack of the ladle. Elisa looked at me in disgust, threw the ladle in the general direction of the sink, and got on her hands and knees.

"Hijo," she said soothingly, taking his head in her hands. "Ernesto."

My cheek ached as I walked toward the living room, leaving mother and son to comfort each other and blame the battered intruder for coming between them. My business with Elisa wasn't quite over but I've been in enough domestic reconciliations to know that I didn't like them and wouldn't be welcome.

Two firemen were working on the hydrant when I stepped out on the porch and picked up my shoes and socks. As I sloshed past them, one of the firemen looked up at me, shook his head, and said, "Kids."

"Kids," I agreed and got into my Crosley wondering if I should stop for a bottle of aspirin.

I wasn't far from Burlington Street so I returned to the scene of the crime and parked in front of Eskian's hardware store. Business wasn't brisk at this hour. Paul Eskian was leaning over his counter, elbow on a bag of fertilizer, reading the morning paper. He scratched his head and looked up at me.

"Looking in the paper for the, the, the murder," he said. "Not here. I figure it might drum up a little, little, little business, bring in a few new customers."

"Might," I said.

"Police were here for hours," he said with a shake of his head. "Hours. Talking to everyone. Even taking, taking pebbles off my roof. Can, can you believe that?"

"I can believe it," I said coming to the counter. "Can you make me an extra key for my Crosley?"

"Sure," he said, reaching out for the key. "Police said you're a private detective."

"The police are right. That OK?"

"Interesting is all," he said.

"When I was in here yesterday," I said, "my car was parked right out there."

"I recall," Eskian said, holding the key up to look at the fine edges.

"You see anyone near my car, maybe in my car?"

"Just you," he said. "And the, the, the guy in the black coat. Noticed because it's too warm for a, a, a coat."

"You tell the police about this guy in the coat?" I asked.

"They didn't ask," said Eskian. "Excuse me."

Eskian turned his back on me and put my Crosley key into his machine.

"Did you get a look at the guy?" I asked, rubbing my sore jaw and considering asking him for an aspirin. "The guy in the black coat?"

"Nope," said Eskian over the sound of the grinding machine. "Could have, have, have been a woman for all I could tell. You aching?"

"Just got hit in the jaw with a ladle."

"Masterson ironware?" he asked.

"I don't know. On the roof," I shouted over the noise, "did you see anything? I mean anybody moving. Anything?"

Eskian turned off the machine, which ground to a screeching halt like fingernails on a blackboard. I shuddered.

"Sorry about, about that," he said blowing steel dust off the key. "Those new machines make, make, make keys but they torture your eardrums every time. That'll be a dime."

I gave him a dime, which he shoved in his pocket rather than opening the cash register.

"Anyone else around who was here yesterday? You mentioned your son."

"Nope," said Eskian apologetically. "Robert was working. Always wanted him in the business with, with me but kids they have a mind of their own, you, you, you know?"

"Right," I said. "What about employees?"

"Got a helper, Keith, but he, he, he wasn't working yesterday," said Eskian. "Anything else I can help you with? Tools, paint, lawn fertilizer?"

"No lawn, nothing to fix," I said. "But I'll be back if I have something broken."

"If they put something in the paper," he said, returning to

the newspaper, "I think I'll clip it out and put it in the window. What do you think? Bad, bad, bad taste?"

"Bad taste," I said pulling out my notebook and writing my number on a sheet. "Here's my number. You think of anything about yesterday that might help, give me a call."

"Will do," he said, jamming the sheet in the pocket with the dime and looking down at the paper.

I left.

I'd been trying to reach Fat Sal Lurtzma for over four hours but the line was always busy. I finally got through just before two in the afternoon. I was in a Rexall drugstore on Hill Street. The phone was near the lunch counter facing a display for enema bags.

"Keep Fit. Keep Clean. Keep Clear for Victory," read the sign above the display. A smiling soldier looked down at the enema bags with something like gratitude.

On the street outside a big red car of the Pacific Electric Railway rumbled by as Sal Lurtzma answered, "You want talent, you've got the number, Sal Lurtzma."

"It's Toby, Sal."

"Toby, I got no time now. I'm expecting a call from Bruckerman in Vegas. I've got a family of jugglers from Poland he's gonna die for."

"I need a theater and a call out for auditions," I said.

"Now you're a producer? Give me a quarter for lunch for Chrissake. Get off the phone. Have a heart, Toby."

My jaw was aching and I had places to go.

"Finish my business and I'll get off the line," I said.

"Talk fast."

"Get a theater and put out a call for Peter Lorre imitators to show up there for an audition tomorrow morning. And put an ad in *Variety*."

"What's the show? This got something to do with the Lorre guy Millman gave me?"

"A movie," I said as a woman in a turban approached as if

she had a call to make. "And it has something to do with the Lorre guy. He's dead. They need a replacement."

"Right. I know Little Augie at the L.A. *Times* and Gonigal on Jimmy Fiddler's radio show. Maybe we can get something in tonight if I hurry. Big question."

"You get fifty bucks," I said.

"Good answer," said Sal. "Get back to me on this one."

I hung up and the turbaned woman trying to look like Maria Montez grabbed for it as I ducked under her arm and the enema display. I found the aspirin display, picked up a bottle, and went to the lunch counter. I was the only customer and the freckle-faced kid in white behind the counter tipped back his white cap and beamed, "What can I do you for?"

"Seltzer, straight," I said, opening the bottle and dropping six or seven aspirin in my palm.

"That stuff can eat right through your stomach lining," said the kid with a shake of his head.

"Seltzer, straight," I repeated.

"Suit yourself," he said with a shrug and moved away while the aspirin began to melt in my moist palm. My jaw ached when I opened my mouth. I wouldn't have minded it too much if I'd had something more to show for it than a couple of beers and a tamale pie lunch.

"Bottoms up," the kid said, placing the clear bubbly glass in front of me. "You like baseball?"

I nodded to indicate that baseball was all right, popped the aspirin, and gulped them down with the entire glass of seltzer while he watched and shook his head.

"My face hurts," I said.

"Hey, none of my business," the kid said, pointing to himself. "It's your stomach. You see where Harris hit a homer in the eleventh yesterday with two on to the beat the Yankees? Boy, the Yankees aren't the Yankees anymore, you know? All those guys going in the army or something."

I looked at the bottle in my hand and considered washing down a few more aspirin.

"I wouldn't," the kid said.

"You ever had real pain kid?" I asked, looking at his freckle-faced Andy Hardy grin.

"Sure," he said.

"Like. . . ?"

"When they amputated my leg," he said, stepping back to pull up his white Rexall trousers to reveal a mold of wood and steel. "Lost it the first day, just outside Pearl Harbor. Never even got to see a Jap."

He let the trouser leg roll down. "More seltzer?" he asked.

"No," I said, putting down a quarter and getting up. "I'll take it easy on the aspirin."

"Good idea," he said, picking up the quarter.

I left the stool wondering whether the kid was a grinner because he was happy to be alive or because he was one of those people who smiled because they had a secret, an important secret that you'd probably never learn and certainly couldn't appreciate.

I was doing a great job with kids this morning. First I'd embarrassed Ernesto in front of his mother and now the Rexall kid had embarrassed me. I figured I might as well get all the kids out of the way in one day so I pulled out my notebook and found the phone number and address for Robert Parotti, the kid assistant to the Steistel brothers. The address was on Union near Seventh.

I went back to the telephone and hovered over Maria Montez, who cupped her hand over the mouthpiece and gave me a go-away look. She was too old to be doing Maria Montez. She smelled OK and might even have looked pretty good if she weren't going out for the wrong role.

"Do you mind?" she asked as I pretended to weigh the merits of major enemas.

"No," I said, and I didn't.

She sighed mightily and went back to her phone call. She

informed somebody named Gaylord that she would have to call him or her back, that she had no privacy, only she pronounced it prih-vah-see. She hung up and glared at me for a beat.

"Sorry I was breathing down your neck, but I was wondering if you'd give me an autograph, Miss Montez," I said, trying to sound shy.

"That is pathetic," she said pronouncing it pah-theh-tic before she high-heeled it down the aisle.

Bobby Parotti wasn't home. A woman, probably his mother, said that it was his day off and he was at the zoo, that Bobby spent all his days off at the zoo. So, I headed for the Griffith Park Zoo after marking the cost of two phone calls and a bottle of aspirin in my back-pocket notebook. I always presented an itemized bill for expenses to my clients. When they questioned it they always did the same thing, picked out the first odd item, like the aspirin. When they got a reasonable answer they didn't ask any more questions even if later there was a twenty-dollar entry for flying lessons.

I'd bodyguarded once for a real estate salesman named Murphy. Murphy's ex-wife had threatened to send her new boy friend around to shake some money out of Murph. Murph had been an Ovaltine box full of good advice.

"When you get the sale about made," he said, "shove the contracts in front of the buyer and tell him to press down hard because you got three carbons. Don't give the customer time to think."

I weighed that advice as I headed for Griffith Park, worked my jaw, and listened to Lorenzo Jones and his wife Belle. Lorenzo and Belle were about to go to bed and she was quoting poetry again. Belle had been quoting quite a bit of poetry recently. I switched to KFWB and listened to the Hollywood Quiz. I got most of the questions. I knew Merle Oberon was married to Alexander Korda who had just been knighted, which meant that Merle was now Lady Korda. I knew Betty Hutton was going to star in *Happy Go Lucky* and that Virginia Weidler was the latest MGM child star. I missed questions about Nelson Eddy and I didn't know Bill Robinson was sixty-four.

It was warm with a threat of rain. Every since the war began, dressing each morning was a guessing game. The papers and the radio couldn't give weather reports because the government was afraid the Japanese would use them. I don't know how. The Japanese probably had weather experts too. Whatever the reason, you didn't know what to expect each day, not that I would have dressed differently.

A thundercloud or two rumbled as I parked in the lot and got out of my car. A pair of sailors and a girl moved past me laughing and got in a Chevy coupe. The zoo was big, and I might not find Parotti but I owed myself a look at some animal faces more homely than mine.

I stopped next to a grassy slope and looked back at the parking lot to be sure no one was tailing me. A car or two parked, people got out, but none of them was familiar and none looked around as if they were trying to spot me. I found a stale piece of Beeman's Pepsin chewing gum in my pocket, unwrapped it, folded it over, and felt it crumble apart between my teeth. When I was satisfied that no one was behind me I headed into the zoo.

The monkey house was the best place to start, not because I knew Parotti like monkeys, but because *I* did. Parotti was there though, sitting on a bench in front of the baboon cage. He had a bag of peanuts and was eating them with total concentration, unaware of his surroundings.

I sat beside him, being careful to avoid a sticky spot, and considered telling him how easily I had found him, maybe saying a few things about telepathy or coincidence or fate or something, but I didn't bother. Unless it happens to you, it doesn't really mean much. You could tell your wife that Hitler was hiding in your basement and she'd say, "Yes dear, did you call my brother and ask to borrow his lawnmower?" It wouldn't be that she didn't believe you. It simply wouldn't register unless she saw Hitler come up the steps sweeping coal dust from his brown uniform and muttering foul-sounding things in German.

"You like the monkeys?" I said.

"Yeah," he answered without looking at me. "But I like the apes more. Baboon's an ape."

He went on eating his peanuts as we watched one of the baboons blink in our direction and then settle down to pick fleas or something out of the hair of another baboon and eat each flea with an intelligent look on his face.

"Smart, they're smart," he said, shaking his head.

People walked past. A few paused to watch the baboons and move on. One soldier with a girl said something to the baboons. The girl with him laughed and clutched his arm.

"They're not funny," said Bobby Parotti.

"They?"

"That soldier. That girl. Not funny at all," he said, turning to look at me for the first time. "I know you?"

"We met on the roof of Eskian's hardware store," I said.

One of the baboons got tired of having fleas picked off his skull and started hooting and chasing the other baboon around the cage. Bars rattled. Baboons bared their teeth. Bobby Parotti's eyes watched the show. His teeth were bared in imitation. The baboons screamed, went eye to eye, and changed their minds. Both retreated to corners of the cage to brood about the stalemate. Bobby closed his mouth.

"Damn," he said. "That was something."

"It was something," I agreed. "The roof of Eskian's," I reminded him.

"Baboons," Bobby said with a knowing shake of his head. "They're like people."

"If you say so, kid," I said. "You remember the roof of Eskian's yesterday?"

Bobby looked at me as if I were mad.

"Sure, I remember. The actor got killed. Pete Lowry.

That's why I've got the day off. They're looking for a replacement. I'm supposed to be looking for a replacement."

"But you're at the zoo," I reminded him.

Bobby shrugged and ate a peanut. He offered me one. I took it and threw it to the baboons. They rushed for it and the bigger one grabbed it first.

"So, they can wait another day," said Bobby.

Seemed reasonable to me. A seventeen-year-old kid was holding up production on a movie because he wanted to watch the baboons in Griffith Park.

"I can help you," I said.

"You don't look like Lowry," Bobby said without bothering to give me a serious look.

"No, but I'm going to be someplace soon where they'll be a lot of Peter Lorres. Trust me. I'll find you someone. Just answer some questions for me."

"Ask," Bobby said looking deeply into his small sack of peanuts. He found one at the bottom, took it out, and began to work on it.

"Who shot Lowry?" I asked.

"You did," he answered. "Cops said it was your gun. That bird woman . . ."

"Mildred Minck," I supplied.

"The one who was hanging around Lowry," he went on. "She said you did it."

"I didn't shoot him," I said.

"OK by me, buddy," he said with a smile. "I didn't much like the guy anyway, and it got me a day off."

"You didn't see anything before Lowry got shot? I mean, on the roof."

"I was watching them do the scene. That's one of my jobs. I watch to see if there's a mistake. I got the script in one hand and I'm watching them with the other. At the same time I'm doing sound."

"You watch with your hands?"

"You know what I mean," he said, crumpling the empty

peanut bag and looking around for a wastebasket. There wasn't one close by so he shoved the bag in his jacket pocket.

"Anybody been bothering Lowry? He have any arguments with anyone?" I asked.

Bobby got up, stretched, looked around for new jungles to conquer, and shook his head negatively.

"Naw, just that Mildred. They were going at it before the setup."

"About what?"

"About what?" he repeated, looking at the baboons for an answer. "Money. Something about money he wanted. And she said something about not liking him doing a love scene with Elisa. She didn't understand the script. It wasn't a love scene. Neiderman is trying to throw her off the roof."

"Neiderman?" I asked.

"The character Lowry was playing," Bobby explained. "That Mildred was nuts. Elisa wouldn't let Lowry touch her finger. Well, I mean, she wouldn't have."

"You like Elisa?" I asked.

He plunged his hands in the pocket of his zipper jacket and looked at me and then away with a blush and a shrug. I went on as three burly young men who looked like Marines on shore leave stopped in front of the cage and began tossing Cracker Jacks at the baboons. Bobby turned his attention to them and frowned. He wasn't going to deal with the puppy love question.

"You ever meet Elisa's son?"

"Ernesto," Bobby said as if he were spitting. "I've met him. He almost hit me."

"Why?" I asked.

The Marines were pelting the baboons, who had backed into a corner of the cage and were clinging to each other and reaching out to gather in an occasional Cracker Jack.

"He didn't like the way I . . . hey, what's this got to do with the price of coffee?"

"Nothing," I said. "The Steistels. How did they get on with Lowry?"

One of the Marines had run out of Cracker Jacks. He looked around for something to pelt the baboons with and picked up a handful of pebbles. Bobby watched the trio and started to shift his weight from leg to leg, his hands plunging more deeply into his pockets.

"What?"

"The Steistels and Lowry," I reminded him.

"I don't know. They didn't talk much in front of me but I had the feeling the old guys didn't like Lowry. They kept talking to him in German. I don't like to hear people talk German. There's a war. You don't use their language."

I couldn't argue with that logic. The Marine with the pebbles began lobbing them at the baboons, who clutched each other in the corner trying to separate pebbles from Cracker Jacks. Bobby was having trouble concentrating on my questions.

"Excuse me," he finally said to me and, hands in pockets, took five or six steps toward the three men laughing in front of the cage.

Bobby said, "Excuse me," again, but this time the words were aimed at the three Marines. They didn't hear him or didn't want to. A couple of old women turned to Bobby, realized they weren't being addressed, and moved on. My sore jaw twinged a warning.

"Bobby," I whispered, but Bobby was on a mission.

"Excuse me," he said louder.

One of the laughing Marines looked over his shoulder.

"Who? Us?" he asked.

"Yes," replied Bobby. "Please leave the baboons alone. How'd you like to have someone throwing things at you in a cage?"

The laughing Marine stopped laughing.

"What's it to you, kid? They your parents?"

One of the other Marines thought this was pretty funny.

The third and biggest of the trio suddenly didn't think anything was funny.

"Just don't bother them, that's all," Bobby said, taking his hands out of his pockets.

I didn't know if baboons ate meat but I had a feeling they might soon be given the opportunity to try tidbits of Bobby Parotti. I sighed, got up, tested my limbs and back, worked my jaw like the tin man in *The Wizard of Oz,* and decided that I was still operating even without an oil can. I moved to Bobby's side as the first Marine took a step toward the boy. Two of the Marines were only a little older than Bobby. The third and biggest was ancient, probably twenty-four or twenty-five.

"You work here or something?" one of the younger Marines asked.

"No," Bobby answered before I could say yes. "I just think you should let them alone."

The Marine marched three steps forward and grabbed Bobby's jacket at the collar. The empty peanut pack came tumbling out of Bobby's pocket. I reached forward, grabbed the Marine's wrist, and twisted down and hard. He pulled back his burned wrist, grabbed it with his other hand and gritted his teeth in my direction. I tried to keep track of the other two Marines, who were stepping forward as I watched the one I had burned, expecting him to make the first move.

I also hoped that someone was watching this and would run for a cop or a keeper. I'd had enough fighting for one day.

But it wasn't the Marine who moved. It was Bobby, who leaped forward and threw a straight right at the young man who stood glaring at me. The punch caught the Marine by surprise. The fist hit the side of his neck and sent him sprawling backward into the arms of the second Marine, who caught him.

"Run, Bobby," I whispered. "Get some help. I'll talk to these guys."

"No," said Bobby, who could have been jammed into the pocket of any one of the three Marines in front of us.

The baboons had moved to the front of the cage and were holding onto the bars, watching us and chattering, showing their teeth and taking odds on Bobby's and my chances for survival.

The two younger Marines moved toward us again and I reached into my pocket for something, anything. A bat would have been nice but all I found was my key chain. I wished I had more keys. I clutched the keys in my right hand and made a fist.

"You leave the monkeys alone," Bobby screamed in near hysteria.

"You got it, kid," said the Marine whose wrist I had twisted. "And so do you, old man."

I figured he was talking to me. I had been expecting a punch, not an insult. He had found the perfect lead. It had come naturally. He went for me as the other Marine reached out for Bobby. My Marine didn't expect much trouble and I wasn't sure how much I could give him in the long run. If I was lucky, I might manage to put a member of the armed forces out of business for weeks or months when he should have been landing on some island with a rifle in his hands. I even had time to think that picking on baboons was less frustrating and dangerous than talking back to drill sergeants or getting shot at. It didn't matter. I ducked as if I were going to try to cover up and minimize the beating I expected. The Marine stepped in front of me and looked down. I couldn't see his face, just his feet, but I could sense where he was hovering. I could hear Bobby shouting, "Bastard," as the second Marine shoved him backward toward the bench. I didn't know where the big Marine was. I shot up suddenly and my head caught the chin of the guy in front of me. As he straightened up with a groan, I threw my key-handed fist into his midsection. He staggered back in pain and I turned to help Bobby or get myself really hurt.

Bobby didn't need any help. The big, older Marine was standing between him and the attacker.

"It's over," said the big guy.

"Not yet," said the guy who had attacked me as he lurched forward, blood trickling from a cut on his chin.

"Albert," the big Marine said deeply, "I said it's over. You read that?"

Albert stopped, looked at the big guy, touched his bloody chin, gave me a look to melt iron, and nodded.

"You OK?" the big guy asked, looking over his shoulder at me.

"I'm OK," I said.

"You OK, kid?" he asked Bobby.

"OK," Bobby said, glaring at the Marine who had pushed him.

"You got guts, buddy," the big guy said. "You and your kid."

"Thanks," I said.

The big guy pointed in the general direction of the lion house and the other two started to walk in that direction.

"Win the war," I said.

"Will do," answered the big Marine, pulling a handkerchief out of his pocket and handing it to his pal with the bloody chin.

The disappointed baboons chattered or jeered at the departing trio as I moved over to Bobby.

"You all right?" I asked.

"He thought you were my father?" Bobby said, straightening his jacket.

"Sorry," I said, putting my keys away.

"My father would have got a gun and shot them," Bobby said, looking at me with a challenge in his voice. He may have been running the Steistel brothers' operation but he was a seventeen-year-old kid and thought like one.

"We all do it our own way," I said. "I don't know which way is best. You could have gotten us both in a hospital."

"Rather be in a hospital than run," he said, looking after the Marines, who were about to turn a corner.

I agreed with him.

"You want a hot dog?" I asked.

"You paying?" asked Bobby.

"On me and my client," I said.

And off we went for hot dogs and Coke and some more talk. He told me what he knew about the Steistels, the dead actor, Mildred, and Elisa, and I told him I'd have a Lowry replacement by Friday. He told me I'd better check with the Steistels to be sure it was OK. I bought him a second hot dog and he told me that he was thinking of joining the navy in August when he was eighteen. I wanted to tell him to wait till they came for him, but I wasn't his father. I grunted and tried to figure out what animal I was smelling. When we were done, I offered Bobby a ride home but he said he was going to stay.

"Birds," he said. "I haven't seen the birds."

I left him and headed back for my car, opened the door, and got in after getting an old jacket from the trunk and placing it on the driver's seat to cover the blood or red paint someone had poured on it while I was in the zoo. I spat on my handkerchief and wiped away the message in red that had been written on the windshield. It was only one word in small letters, Stop, but it turned my handkerchief a deep red.

9

It was nearly two when I drove into No-neck Arnie's garage not far from the Farraday.

Arnie was in his overalls working on an Oldsmobile coupe in the corner of the big concrete and brick building. He was covered with grease and cursing to himself as I walked up to him and he pulled his head out of the hood.

"Automatic transmissions," he spat. "Whoever thought the damn things up should be pickled and fried."

"Doesn't sound too appetizing," I told him.

"It's not meant to be. What's your problem?"

"Bad back. Not much money. Sore jaw. Ex-wife who doesn't want to see me. Brother who—"

"With the car," Arnie sighed. Arnie never liked jokes unless he made them.

"Blood or paint all over the front seat," I said.

He wiped his hands on a greasy towel, strode past me to my Crosley, and opened the door.

"It's blood," he said.

"What kind?" I asked.

"How the hell should I know? I'm a mechanic, not a pathologist," he grunted. "Five bucks I'll have my man Buttrick scrub it out. Have it ready in . . . I don't know. An hour, maybe less, if you don't mind it a little damp."

"Three bucks," I said.

"Tell you what, Toby. Buy yourself some Super Suds in the blue and white box, mix it in a pail with hot water, pull out the car seat, and scrub it yourself. Then let it sit in the sun and dry for three, four hours."

"Five bucks," I said.

"You got it," Arnie answered.

"You don't bargain very well, Arnie," I said.

"I get by," he answered with a shrug. "You want me to fill it with gas?"

"Why not? I'll be back in an hour, maybe two. Maybe longer," I said heading for the door.

"I'll be here," called Arnie.

I walked the three blocks to the Farraday. The rain threat had passed and the sky was bright. It was June in Los Angeles. A billboard on Main called out for me to buy an extra war bond in June to help build the Cruiser *Los Angeles*. A drawing of the proposed *Los Angeles* streaked through the water toward Main Street. It was near this corner on December 17, 1870, that a Frenchman named Lachenais had been caught after committing murder. I knew, because my brother Phil had written a paper on unknown crimes in Los Angeles history when he was a student in Glendale High. Before he had written the paper, Phil had taken me with him on a research trip to downtown Los Angeles, which was, at the time, a foreign country to me. I liked the smells, the hustle, the crowds, the big, dark buildings with strange-looking people coming out of them. It was nothing like Glendale. I wanted to live right there on Main Street.

I remembered Phil's paper on Lachenais as I headed for Hoover. Lachenais, angry that a man named Bell had stolen water from him, shot Bell dead. Bell's body was found with no hint of who might have killed him. A few days later Lachenais, seriously drunk, suggested to a neighborhood vigilante that it was a mistake to go riding toward Sonoma in search of the killer.

The vigilante and his pals put things together and marched a now sober Lachenais to the corral of Tomlinson and Griffith at the corner of Temple and New High and hanged him. Phil had written a full page on three-ring lined paper supporting the idea of public hanging for murderers, using Lachenais as his principal example. Phil's high school history teacher hadn't thought much of his choice of subject, his research, or his argument, but it remained a favorite of mine not because of the subject but the fact that Phil had actually taken me with him somewhere and displayed genuine enthusiasm about something, even if it was a hanging.

When I hit Hoover, I imagined a posse including me, Phil, Jeremy, Gunther, and Shelly finding the guy who had sent me the dead pigeon, taken the shot at me, and bloodied my Crosley, and hanging him from a palm tree in Pershing Square.

When I hit the Farraday, I imagined catching the guy myself and tying him down in Shelly's dental chair so Dr. Minck could work on his molars.

I climbed the stairs and went into the office. The lights were out. They should have been on. I turned them on. I can't say the place was any more of a mess than it usually was. The mess was just arranged differently. Shelly should have been in his chair reading old dental journals, dreaming of land deals and rainbow dyes for teeth, chomping on his cigar, but he wasn't there.

What was there was an envelope on the dental chair, a big brown envelope with the single word "Peters" printed on it in black ink. I walked over to the dental chair, picked up the envelope, and sat down. The chair reeked of Shelly's cheap cigars. I turned the envelope over a few dozen times and looked at my printed name. I recognized the printing. I'd seen it in the capsule tied to the leg of the dead pigeon. I'd seen it on the windshield of my car. I opened the envelope and pulled out Shelly's glasses and a sheet of paper on which was neatly written, "We have the dentist. You want him alive, you stop looking. You stop looking, we let him go." It wasn't signed. I slipped the note back in the envelope and moved to my office and the phone.

"Captain Pevsner," Phil answered wearily.

"Private Peters," I said. "Anything new on the Lorre killings?"

"Toby," Phil said slowly with false patience. "We don't have Lorre killings. We've got some unrelated acts of violence which coincidentally happen to involve people who, among other things, do imitations of Peter Lorre. It's not all that coincidental either. I've seen you do Peter Lorre imitations. Anyone trying to kill you?"

"Yeah," I said, "but not because I do a lousy Peter Lorre. I do a lousy John Wayne and a miserable Victor McLaglen. You've heard my Victor McLaglen? 'Sorry for your troubles, Mrs. McPhillip,'" I said with an Irish brogue that sounded pretty weak to me.

Phil was silent on the other end.

"That the official line from city hall?" I asked. "The Lorre business is a series of coincidences?"

"Something like that," Phil agreed.

"And you're . . ."

"Holding onto a job," Phil said.

"Not like you, Phil," I said. "You've never done what the boys in the hall have told you to do."

"Shit," hissed Phil. "I've got a wife, three kids, house payments, old hospital bills. I'm fifty-three years old and my kids are going to want to go to college."

"How do you know?" I asked, looking around my office and then turning in my chair to look out of my window to the alley below.

"Because I'm going to tell them to go, that's why," he shouted. "Get off the damned phone. I've got work to do, some unrelated cases to solve."

"Like . . ."

"Like a woman named Gumbatz, Lucille Gumbatz who was shot at last night in the Morocco Bar while she was doing an imitation of Peter Lorre."

Two bums in the alley were tugging at a discarded chair.

One bum had the legs, the other had the back. They tugged and probably yelled. I couldn't tell. The window was closed and they were too far away. All I could hear was the traffic on Hoover and Ninth.

"Thanks, Phil," I said.

"I've got work," he croaked.

"I've got information," I said and told him about the pigeon, the shot fired at me, the blood in my car, and the note about Shelly.

"Bring in the note, the pigeon, and your car," he said. "We'll have the police lab go over them."

"Threw the pigeon in a trash can on Fourteenth Street and the car's being washed. You can have the kidnaping note. I'll drop it off."

"I'll put Seidman on the Minck kidnaping if it is a kidnaping. Minck's probably pulling something to make his old lady sorry for him. Anything else?"

"My gun," I said.

"Forget it," he answered.

"Lachenais," I said. "You remember him?"

"I remember him," said Phil. "He never died. He had a hundred kids and they had a hundred kids and they're all nuts and loose in the city and I've got to get off the phone and round them up. Good-bye."

He hung up and I played with Shelly's glasses while I watched the two bums in the alley pull the old chair apart. Each bum held his useless half of a chair ready to use it as a weapon. They stood threatening. I bet on the shorter bum who had the back of the chair and looked more determined, but I never found out. The other bum threw his half of the chair in the air and walked away in disgust. The little bum retrieved the piece and tried to put it together with his own.

I pocketed the glasses, got up and went into Shelly's office, looked around for something, anything, found nothing, turned out the lights and left. I locked the door and went down the stairs, knowing that Shelly's best chance of being found was through me. The threat didn't make sense. How long could the killer hold Shelly? When he let Shelly go, I'd come after him. His threats hadn't stopped me. Eventually, he'd either have to let Shelly go, which wasn't likely, take care of him forever, which wasn't likely, or kill him, which seemed the most likely.

I left the Farraday and wandered down to Hill and Arnie's garage.

The Crosley was parked in front of the building. The windshield was clean and the seats were clean but wet. The keys weren't in the car. I found Arnie inside eating a sandwich on the hood of the Oldsmobile whose transmission he was working on. The white bread sandwich had greasy fingerprints on it but Arnie didn't seem to notice. I paid him and he tossed me my key.

"Someone kidnaped Shelly," I said.

"Tough," replied No-neck Arnie. "You need a tune-up."

"They may kill him," I said.

"These are hard times," answered Arnie around a mouthful of salami, wilted lettuce, and bread. "You could use a tire rotation too."

"You'd make a great general, Arnie," I said, heading for the door.

"I've been miscast by life," he said, reaching for a thermos in which any possible liquid might be sloshing. "But I try to make the best of a small role."

"You're a philosopher, Arnie," I said, opening the street door and letting in daylight.

"We've all got hidden depths," he answered. "You want to bring the car in for the tune-up and tire change?"

"When I find Shelly," I called out.

"Hey, life goes on," he shouted back. "You want some extra gas coupons? Price is down. Five bucks a book."

"I'll think about it," I shouted again and closed the door.

My best chance of getting Shelly back alive wasn't to give up on the Lorre case. My best chance was to solve the Lorre

case and find the killer who had Shelly—if Shelly were still
alive when I found him.

It wasn't that late. When I got in the car, my watch said it
was nine, which could have meant it was any time. The watch
hadn't worked since my father left it to me. I'd never thought
about fixing it, never thought about putting it in a drawer.
The handles turned. The watch ticked. I wound it and wore it.

The radio told me it was almost five. Normally, I'd start
thinking about food, but this wasn't normally. I put Shelly's
glasses on the narrow dashboard, dragged out my notebook,
found out where the Steistels lived, and pulled into traffic.

I dropped the envelope off for my brother at the Wilshire
police station. I didn't hang around to see him. He was getting too mellow and I didn't have the time to prod him into a
rage. My appetite did come back when I passed Ahrens on
Wilshire. I found a parking space too near the corner and put
a card on the dashboard indicating that I was a California
State Health Inspector—On Duty.

Ahrens was crowded but there were a few spaces for singles. I found one and got the Special Complete Dinner—
chicken soup, roast beef, two vegetables, ice cream, butter-
milk, and a boiled potato—for sixty-five cents. I ate fast, left
a dime tip, and fifteen minutes later I was parked in front of
Miracle Films.

Miracle Films was on Alvarado near Echo Park. Miracle
Films was not easy to find. Miracle Films did not have a studio or an office building. Miracle Films had a narrow entrance
wedged between a small grocery and an exterminator's. The
name Miracle Pictures was neatly written on a card taped
above a brass bell. The card was dirty.

I pushed the bell. Nothing. I pushed again and heard a
latch click in the wooden door. I pushed the door open and
stepped in. The stairway was narrow and went almost straight
up into near darkness. I walked up holding the wooden railing
and moving toward a faint light. The wooden stairs creaked
and yawned and I moved ever upward till I found myself in

front of a door. There was no landing, just a door with a pebbled glass square window on which was printed Miracle Pictures in peeling gold ink outlined in peeling black. The door opened before I could reach for the knob and Gregor Steistel stood looking down at me. He was chewing on something and had a napkin tied around his neck. He wore the same shabby suit he'd worn on the roof of Eskian's hardware store.

"Yes?" he said suspiciously.

"Peters," I said.

He squinted at me and stopped chewing. Nothing came to him so he started chewing again.

"I was on the roof when Kindem got shot," I explained.

"Kindem?"

"Lowry," I said.

"The police have talked already to Eric and me about this," he said, swallowing whatever he'd been chomping on.

"I've got other questions," I said. "Can I come in?"

"In?" He asked and looked back into "in."

"I can help you," I said. "I think I can get you a replacement for Lowry."

Something like hope came over his lined face, and passed.

"That is Bobby's responsibility," he said.

"I've talked to Bobby. You want my cooperation on this, you give me a few answers."

"I'll have to ask my brother," Gregor said, closing the door.

I leaned against the glass pane with my ear to it but all I could make out was two voices arguing in what was probably German. Then came a pause followed by a machine-gun burst of German and then silence again. Footsteps in my direction. I pulled my ear from the glass and stepped down with my hands plunged into my jacket pocket.

The door opened again and Gregor motioned me in and stood back holding the door so I could pass. Miracle Pictures' reception area was not impressive. The high-ceilinged "room" was wide and not really a room at all but the front part of an attic which had been curtained off from the rest of the space by a canvas curtain. The unfinished wood floor was bare except for a badly worn oriental rug of doubtful nationality. A wooden table stood in front of the door with a chair behind it. Two other unmatched chairs were in the space but they didn't face the deck. On the table were piles of papers and newspapers and something that looked like a gutted movie camera.

The room ran the width of the building and made the chairs and table look like an afterthought. The only touch of color came from the movie posters taped to the plaster walls, and they weren't particularly colorful.

"This way," Gregor said, walking to the canvas curtain.

"I was just admiring your posters," I said politely, following him.

"The posters," Gregor said, looking around at the walls as if he were seeing them for the first time. "Yes. They represent many years of work for Eric and me. Years of work in Europe and here."

I looked around at the posters. Four or five were in German and looked a little grisly. One displayed a green, hulking man in a cloak holding a long knife dripping green blood. The movie was, apparently, called *Der Sturm*. The others were no less threatening, including the French one with the man strangling a woman or a man with long hair. The American movies, three of them, were *Secrets of Darkness, Terror at Midnight* and *The White Ghost*. All of the posters were green or blue and filled with murder and shadows.

"You are familiar with our work?" Gregor asked.

"I think I saw that one," I said, pointing at the *Secrets of Darkness* poster.

"Ah, yes," he said with a knowing smile. "The dream film, the nightmare film. You know of course that Eric was a founder of film expressionism. He worked for Heinrich Galeen on *The Golem* and Weine on *Das Cabinet of Dr. Cal-*

igari and I, I was an assistant cameraman on *Warning Shadows.*"

"That a fact?" I said.

"But times are hard now," Gregor said, looking toward a poster. "Now, to survive we must produce dreck. You know 'dreck'?"

"Intimately," I said.

"Bring him in," came Eric's voice from beyond the curtain. "We do not exist to bore visitors with tales of our lost past. Bring him in. Bring him in. Bring him in."

Gregor brought me in through a slit in the canvas that was hidden by the draping of the fabric.

"In" was not much better than "out."

The space behind the curtain was the size of a basketball court, though only the area to half court was lighted. In the darkness beyond, I could make out the shape of painted boards stacked up, light stands, a few tripods and cameras, and some cabinets. In the lighted space in which I was standing were the living quarters of the Steistel brothers—two beds next to each other against one wall with an ornate chest of drawers next to each bed, a couple of wooden wardrobes with doors open to reveal the suits, shirts, and other clothing of the two old men, a round, heavy wooden table with two candle holders in the center and four chairs around it. Add to that a sofa and two stuffed chairs, none of which matched. On the opposite wall was a stove with something bubbling on it, and a refrigerator.

Eric Steistel was sitting at the table with a plate of food in front of him. His sightless eyes were aimed more or less in my direction.

"Sorry to come during dinner, but this is important," I said.

"Gregor says you are able to find a replacement for Lowry."

"I think so. An agent friend and I are looking."

"And why do you do this?" asked Eric with a knowing little

smile. "What commission do you hope to gain? We are not a big studio. We can pay at best . . ."

He said something to Gregor in German and Gregor answered.

". . . at best," Eric went on, "five hundred dollars to the actor. We have one more week of shooting. Of course, payment will be deferred until we have a distribution and you, you will receive twenty-five dollars. Gregor can prepare a contract."

"No contract, no commission," I said. "Can I sit?"

"I do not know if you are capable of sitting," said Eric. "But you may sit if you can."

I sat near the table.

"You've got a sense of humor," I said.

"Eric always was known for his wit," said Gregor, going for the pot on the stove and turning off the flame. "He was known in Berlin at UFA Studio as the comical expressionist."

"The sardonic expressionist," said Eric wearily as if he had corrected his brother hundreds of times before, which he probably had. "You'd like some goulash, Mr. . . ."

"Peters," I said. "No thanks. I ate before I got here. But you go ahead."

Gregor poured goulash into the two bowls on the table, tore bread off the loaf in front of him, and put one chunk in Eric's hand. I waited while they ate after Gregor stopped me from speaking with a finger to his lips.

I waited and listened to the two old men eating, Eric looking nowhere and Gregor looking from me to his brother. They ate slowly and I sat patiently. When he was finished, Eric pushed his plate away and turned in my general direction.

"And so, Mr. Peters, we resume our conversation," said Eric.

"Someone killed Lowry," I reminded them.

"Of that we are painfully aware," sighed Eric.

Eric tapped the table lightly with his fingertips as Gregor began to clear the table.

"Lowry said 'Steinholtz' just before he died," I said, cutting into Eric's sightless memories of expressionism in good old Berlin. "You never heard the name?"

Eric laughed like a pebble in a tin can.

"Steinholtz," he rasped. "How many Steinholtzes have we known, Gregor?"

Gregor paused at the sink to consider the question seriously.

"Steinholtz, the baker who wanted to write poetry," answered Gregor. "I think he shot his dog and himself in 1920 or '23. Then there was Steinholtz the eye doctor. Only he wasn't an eye doctor and his name wasn't really Steinholtz. He took that name from his cousin because his name was Greenberg and he thought . . ."

"I get the idea," I said.

"Steinholtz is a common name in Germany," said Gregor, going back to his dishes.

"Was Lowry German?" I asked.

"Perhaps," said Gregor. "He spoke German."

"Definitely," said Eric triumphantly. "He had the pretend accent to simulate Lorre, but beneath the pretend accent was a real accent. He claimed to be a cousin of the real Peter Lorre, but . . ."

"How did he get the role?" I asked, as Gregor examined a stubborn goulash stain on one of the plates.

"An agent," said Eric.

"No," corrected Gregor. "Elisa brought him to us."

"Elisa knew Lowry?" I asked. "Where . . ."

"Music," Eric said suddenly, as if ordering a studio orchestra into action. Gregor responded by turning off the running water, drying his hands on a dish towel, and moving to one of the dressers, where he removed a purple cloth from an old record player. A stack of records stood neatly alongside the old Victor machine. Eric drummed his fingers expectantly on the table and I said, "Where did Elisa. . . ?"

"Not now. Not now," Eric said impatiently, putting his fingers to his lips to silence me.

Gregor selected a disk, blew on it gently, and placed it on the turntable. The Steistel Brothers were not to be rushed. I looked around the dark loft for some closet where Shelly might be stored, but saw nothing.

The machine crackled and I expected something Wagnerian. I got a hot, unexpected blast of loud trumpet that lightninged through my head.

"Harry James," Eric whispered reverently during a slight break in the solo. "'Trumpet Blues and Cantabile.'"

"Harry James," Gregor added seriously just before the band blasted out again into the dark corners of the loft, "has just been voted the best lead trumpet in the country in the *Metronome* poll."

"And," screamed Eric with delight over the blast of brass, "second only to Ziggy Elman as best hot trumpet. And do not forget *Downbeat*'s poll had Harry James as favorite soloist."

"Who could forget," I called over a crescendoing riff.

"Listen, listen, listen," Eric shouted, cocking his head to one side. "James's trumpet calls the trumpet section to play the blues over this bouncing upbeat tempo. Now. There. Now." He bounced in his chair excitedly. "Suddenly everything smooths out as the strings play this long bridge back to Harry James's lead trumpet in a hot, melodic chorus. Listen."

We listened. Gregor stood at attention, guarding the machine. I knew a headache was on the way if I didn't escape.

"I think . . ." I began.

"Now," Eric cried excitedly, "the boogie beat brings back the blues motif, and the brass soars to a triumphant climax."

We listened to the triumphant climax and then the record ended. Eric sank back exhausted. Gregor gently removed the record and addressed me.

"You would like some Charlie Shavers?" he asked, sounding more like a waiter suggesting dessert than a German cameraman offering pain to an aching head.

"I don't . . ." I began.

"'Saint Louis Blues,'" Eric jumped in. "Magnificent backup by Buster Bailey on clarinet."

"Or you might prefer," Gregor went on, "'Bugle Blues' with Buck Clayton on trumpet. Excellent Count Basie arrangement."

"No, thanks," I got in. "I've got a little headache and I'd like some information. Remember?"

Gregor nodded and went to the stove where he poured two cups of coffee. I resumed talking before Eric could launch into a tribute to Charlie Shavers.

"A dentist has been kidnaped," I said.

"Why?" asked Eric. "Who would pay ransom for a dentist?"

"It's not for ransom. It's to keep me from looking for whoever killed Lowry and another Peter Lorre imitator."

"Mr. Lowry was not an imitator," Eric said indignantly, turning to face my general direction. "He was an impressionist, an artist."

"Artists work cheap these days," I said, looking around the dark, windowless loft.

"We could afford far better than this," Gregor said at the sink as he poured me a cup of coffee. "But we are living frugally and investing our money."

"In movies," Eric whispered, in case the Warner Brothers had their ears to the door. "We are saving our own movies, buying the rights to other low-budget features that have already been shown in theaters."

"Why?" I asked accepting the coffee cup from Gregor. "What can you do with old B movies?"

"Television," shouted Eric triumphantly.

"Television?" I repeated, wondering how I could get rid of

the headache and get back on the subject of Shelly's kidnaping.

"Klaus Landsberg . . ." Eric began.

"We knew him in Germany, an electrical genius," added Gregor as I hurried through the coffee.

"Klaus was hired last year by Paramount Studios to organize and operate a new experimental television station," said the excited Eric who was, once again, addressing the wall. "That will make two stations operating in Los Angeles, Paramount's and Don Lee's."

"So?" I asked.

"Soon there will be five, six stations," said Eric growing ever more excited. "And people will be buying receiving machines. Hundreds . . ."

"Thousands," entered Gregor from the sink.

"Ten thousand," Eric raised in the poker game of dreams.

"A hundred thousand," countered Gregor.

"And they will need something to put on the television, something to see," beamed the blind man.

"Old movies?" I guessed.

"Precisely," said Eric.

"Never happen," I said, getting up. "People aren't going to sit around their living rooms in the dark watching old movies they wouldn't go see in a theater."

"We shall see," said Eric, which struck me as ironic coming from a blind man. "I am a bit of a Cassandra. I can see the future but no one but Gregor believes me. Therefore, my brother and I will profit from my skill at prophesy."

"Good luck," I said, heading for the curtain.

"We shall use our profits to make films," Eric shouted, sensing or hearing me move away, "films in the great tradition of expressionism. I have vision, Mr. Peters. The dark shadows of the past, of our psyches, shall be unleashed through the artistry of the soul in image and sound. We shall reveal the deepest horrors of the human spirit. We shall make visible what our repressions have told us should forever be kept secret. We shall liberate the monsters of our libidos and stand them naked before us in the theater of illusion."

"Sounds like fun to me," I said.

"What about the replacement for Lowry?" Eric shouted even louder as I groped for the opening in the canvas.

"Maybe tomorrow. Maybe Saturday," I said as Gregor hurried over to find the break in the canvas for me and part it.

I looked over at Eric before I left. His sightless eyes were aimed into the darkness of the studio and he was smiling.

"Gregor," he called. "'C Jam Blues' followed by a little Elman, perhaps 'Moonlight on the Ganges.'"

Gregor gave me an apologetic little nod that let me know I should find my own way out. I nodded back to show it was fine with me, and I stepped into the reception area and crossed the space to the door. As I opened the door to Miracle Pictures, I heard the first blare of Billy Strayhorn's trumpet.

I made my way down the dark, narrow stairwell with Duke Ellington following close behind, pounding with both elegant hands on my head. When I opened the street door, the afternoon sun blinded me. I stood for a few seconds till I could see again and realized that my headache had become a heavyweight contender.

Thinking sometimes gives me headaches and I had been thinking too much lately, but I didn't want to take any of the credit away from the Steistel brothers' concert. I didn't seem to be getting closer to Lowry's killer and Shelly's kidnaper. Maybe Seidman and my brother were having better luck but I doubted it.

My head was throbbing too hard for me to consider driving and the sun was breathing down on me too hot for me to see clearly. I made my way through the door of a Greek restaurant across the street, checked to be sure it was empty, and went into the welcome darkness and silence. It was perfect. An old man with bushy hair and walrus mustache dyed black escorted me to a table near an open space that looked like a miniature dance floor. He poured water for me into a green glass and stood back.

"Greek coffee and a generous slice of baclava," I said softly. He smiled and walked away without a word and, mercifully, without a clattering of feet. I pulled out my aspirin, inhaled half a bottle washed down with water, and sank back in the cool silence with my eyes closed.

The horror was sudden, worthy of Eric Steistel's worst or best images from hell. A brass horn blasted in my ear and someone shouted, "Whoopah." My eyes opened in pain to the sight of three people standing in front of me, two ancient men and a creature of no known gender or age. They all wore suits. One of the men held a cornet. The other man had an accordion. The maybe-woman held a mandolin. I don't know which one of them had yelled, but I do know that they grinned at me, stomped their feet explosively on the wooden floor, shouted, and played their instruments.

The second wave of horror came with the realization that they were performing for me. There was no one else in the place but the old waiter, and he seemed to have been smart enough to take off for Boyle Heights. I was wrong. He appeared just as the trio finished whatever they were playing and screaming and started on another tune of no identifiable melody. I tried to smile through the pain as I drank my coffee. I tried to ignore them as they launched into a Greek version of 'Johnny Got a Zero' while I ate my baclava. My fingers grew sticky from honey. I licked them, waved them in the air, and tried a weary "Whoopah" of my own, figuring it could only burst a vessel in my brain and release me from this mortal coil. And there was some chance it might slow the musicians down.

My next ploy was to smile and point to my head, to which the mandolin player responded with a Greek version of something that might once have been Beethoven. At that point, rudeness and a run for the door seemed the only chance I had to avoid permanent brain damage. I started to get up but the old waiter with the dyed hair came back and motioned for the trio to stop. They did and I considered giving the old guy a kiss on each cheek.

But he hadn't come to rescue me.

"Telephone," he said.

"For me?" I asked, popping the last crumb of baclava in my mouth.

"You Mr. Peters?" he asked.

"Yeah."

"For you," he said and pointed to the cashier's counter near the door where a phone sat off the hook.

The trio watched and waited. I dropped a buck on the table and pointed at it and them. I don't know why I assumed they couldn't speak English but I did.

I lurched to the phone and picked it up.

"Hello," I said.

"We've been watching you," came a voice that could be coming from a woman, a nervous kid, or a man doing a rotten imitation of Mickey Mouse.

"I hope you've enjoyed the show so far, but I hear Hedy Lamarr in *Ecstasy* is worth a trip to the Aztec Theater."

"This is no joke," screamed Mickey Mouse.

The old waiter came over to the counter, handed me the bill for the coffee and baclava, and looked at my face.

"Headache?" he mouthed.

I nodded yes as Mickey Mouse screamed in my ear. The waiter held up a stubby finger, turned, and disappeared again.

"What do you want?" I asked. "I've got a headache."

"I'm sorry," said Mickey. "But we warned you."

"Nobody warned me about this headache," I said.

"Not the headache," the voice squealed again. "The investigation. We warned you."

"You tried to goddamn kill me," I countered.

"No," the caller whined. "Warnings, just warnings. For God's sake this isn't easy on us . . ."

"Hey, I'm sorry," I said looking back into the restaurant. The band was gone, faded into the paneling, under the tables, into the Greek town painted on the wall, or wherever they lurked, waiting for their victims.

"Stop investigating," came the voice. "Or we'll kill the dentist. We will. We saw you go to Miracle Pictures. We'll kill him."

"I went for coffee and some Harry James," I said. "Look, if you have something to say, say it. I've got work to do."

"Minck," he screamed.

"What makes you think I give a damn what you do with him?" I said, trying to sound as indifferent as Ned Sparks. "I've got a real problem here. You ever have a headache? I mean a real headache that tears off the side of your skull?"

"No," came the voice. "Once when I was . . ."

"Forget it," I said. "This is my headache. I don't want to hear your sad stories."

"Be reasonable," the voice cried.

"OK," I said. "I'll be reasonable. You kill him and I keep up the investigation till it leads me to you and I kill you. You let him go and I continue the investigation till it leads to you and I don't kill you. I just turn you over for murder."

"That's not a very good choice," came the Mickey voice.

"It's not supposed to be," I said, biting my lower lip to hold back the pain in my head. "You killed two people, hurt another one. Kidnaped a dentist, which may or may not be a crime in California, and you took a shot at me, not to mention murdering a pigeon and ruining my car."

"Mistakes happen," the voice said. "They can happen to anyone. It wasn't supposed to go like this."

"I'm hanging up," I said.

"Wait . . ."

"Wait for what?" I asked.

The caller put the phone down on something hard. I listened, heard nothing, and watched the old waiter weave his way toward me between tables with a fresh glass of water in one hand and something in the open palm of the other.

"Toby?" Shelly's voice bellowed on the phone.

"Yes, Shel," I said.

"I've been kidnaped," he said.

"I figured that out, Shel. They even left a note."

"These are not kind people, Toby. Not kind at all," Shelly bleated.

The old waiter held out his left hand, on which there rested seven round, green capsules. I took all seven and he gestured for me to put them in my mouth.

"Hold on, Shel," I said. "I'm taking some pills for my headache."

"Headache," he cried. "Headache. I'm being threatened with . . . with . . ." and then, to whoever it was on the other side, "What are you threatening me with, cutting off my hands, torture, murder?"

"Shelly," I said through the pills rattling in my mouth. "They don't need your suggestions."

I took the water, washed down the pills and handed the glass back to the waiter.

"Where are you, Sheldon?" I asked.

"Where am . . . a basement, something. How do I know? They took my glasses. Toby, do what they tell you to do for my sake. For Mildred's sake. She's too young to be a widow."

I figured her for just about the right age but I asked Shelly, "How many of them are there?"

"Two," he said. "They jumped me in the office. I was just going to clean up the place when they came in. I swear as God is my witness, I was going to clean up."

"Who are they, Shel?" I asked.

"I don't know," he cried. "You think I know kidnapers and murderers? I'm a dentist. I've never seen these people before. Without my glasses I can't see them now. Will you just do what they want? Will you do that for me?"

"Describe them, Shel," I said. "Do it fast."

"Well . . ." he began, "the older one . . ." and someone pulled the phone away from Shelly and screamed like Mickey Mouse.

"That's not fair, Peters. That is not fair here. We've been square with you. I owe you that, but you've got to take this seriously."

"I don't think I've got anything else to talk to you about. Remember, you hurt the dentist, I find and hurt you."

"It wasn't supposed to go like this," the caller cried.

I hung up.

"Well?" asked the waiter, clasping his hands together as if I were going to report on the birth of twins.

My headache wasn't gone but it was going.

"Old Greek remedy?" I asked.

"Chinese," he said. "Yin Chao. Get it from Chau Ling's in Chinatown. Great stuff. Don't know what's in it."

"Thanks," I said.

"My pleasure," the waiter said, touching his mustache.

I walked out into the street. The sun didn't hurt nearly as much now, thanks to Yin Chao and the knowledge that I was getting someplace.

10

The day wasn't exactly young, but it wasn't old either, and I had work to do and some leads to follow. I went back to my office. It wasn't close but it beat going back to Mrs. Plaut's. It was after five when I got there, so there were parking spaces on the street. I looked around for whoever was tailing me but I didn't see him, which meant that he was either very good or I wasn't being watched at the moment.

It was clear that the guy with the Mickey Mouse voice hadn't been following me. He had been somewhere with Shelly and a telephone. Whoever was following me had called Mickey Mouse, told him the name of the Greek restaurant, and told him to call. If Mickey Mouse were the brains of the outfit, I was riding high in the saddle, an expression I picked up from a Buck Jones movie. I've only been on a horse once in my life and I didn't like it. The horse had liked it even less.

The Farraday lobby was empty, but that didn't surprise me. There were no sounds echoing through the well-scrubbed hallways, which didn't surprise me either. The usual sounds of the Farraday were muffled, faintly musical, and came from the offices that lined the hallways on each floor. I trudged up the stairway, listening to the early evening calm, and pausing to be sure no footsteps were behind me.

When I hit the fourth floor, my legs were feeling a little weak. I credited my recent headache, my bout with Elisa's son Ernesto, Shelly's kidnaping and an all-around hell of a day. I didn't want to think about my legs being half a century old, but I couldn't help it. I tried to think of nothing. My Farraday landlord, the wrestling poet Jeremy Butler, had once tried to teach me to meditate, to think of nothing. It seemed easy when he suggested it, and then I tried. I had just about come to the conclusion that it isn't possible to think of nothing when my mind went blank one afternoon while I was sitting at my desk looking at a crack in the wall and waiting for a miracle. That blankness was clean, simple, and lasted about half an hour that felt like a few seconds. When a thought came back, I tried to find that blankness again, but I couldn't. I never did find it again.

When I opened the door to Shelly's and my office, I wasn't thinking about meditating. I was thinking about why the door wasn't locked. I was sure I'd locked it. Something moved inside the dark dental office beyond the tiny waiting room I was standing in. My gun was somewhere in the evidence room of the Wilshire police station. Whoever was in there had heard me coming in. There was no covering that. I pulled the chain on the light in the waiting room, started to hum "Ramona" as casually as I could, and leaned down to remove the wooden leg of one of the two chairs in the waiting area. It had been more than a year since I'd told Shelly to fix the chair, warned him that some day a patient would sit on it and break a limb or two, but Shelly had cast his thoughts beyond waiting room chairs. I held the chair leg tightly in my right hand and eased the dismantled chair against the little table covered with old magazines. Then I got up, opened the door to Shelly's office, and stepped in ready to swing, jump, or run. There was no one there.

Maybe there was no one there. Maybe I was imagining things. Maybe I had left the door open and maybe I had even left the Arvin radio on the shelf near the sink on, but I didn't think so. Armed and ready, I moved to the sink and reached up to turn off the radio—and got a better idea. I turned the volume up. Gabriel Heatter's voice came on with some good news and some bad. The United States, Great Britain, and Russia had pledged to open a new front in Europe, with the United States hitting the mainland. The Germans were being hit hard on the Russian front. According to the Russians, the Germans had lost 15,000 soldiers, fifty tanks and eighty planes in the Crimea in just three days. The bad news was that there were reports that the Japanese had landed or were about to land in the Aleutian Islands.

I didn't have time for more news. I moved to my office door, reached down quietly with my Neanderthal club at the ready, and threw open the door.

Elisa stifled a scream. She was standing at the window smoking. She dropped the cigarette and looked at the club-wielding shadow figure who had burst into the room.

"Don't," she cried.

"I'm not," I said lowering the chair leg. "What are you doing here? How did you get in?"

She leaned against my desk with one hand on her chest, between her breasts, trying to catch her breath.

"I got in because I told an Amazon woman who said she was the landlord's wife that I was a client, and I had to wait for you. She said she didn't want me waiting in the halls, that it wasn't safe to wander the halls of the Farraday after dark. I wouldn't doubt it."

"That was Alice Pallis Butler," I said. "She's a romantic. Her husband's a poet."

"I wouldn't want to be her husband and get into a fight with her over who was doing the dishes," Elisa said.

"He's even bigger than she is," I said, closing the door and putting the chair leg on the end of my desk. "And they don't fight. They're in love."

"That's nice," Elisa said, her breath neatly caught.

Her hair was dark, fluffy, and long and her face made up, not movie made up but made up. She wore a gray dress that showed a lot of shapely frontage. Her shoulders were padded and she looked like she'd just stepped into the detective's office in a Mike Shayne movie.

"You need help?" I asked, standing across the desk from her.

"I brought you something," she said, and pointed a scarlet fingernailed finger at a package about the size of a cigar box on the desk.

"Thanks," I said reaching for the package. It was neatly wrapped and tied. I moved around the desk past her, smelled her spicy scent, and fished in my mess of a desk drawer for a knife. I found my Boy Scout knife with the broken handle and cut the strings on the package. The paper fell open like a tulip and a sweet almond smell came out.

"Careful," she said. "Flan."

I carefully opened the rest of the package and found myself looking at a dish of brownish jelly. She had even included a spoon. I took the spoon and tasted the flan. It was sweet.

"You just making the rounds of detective offices, barber shops, churches and boys' clubs spreading good cheer and flan, or am I a special project?" I asked, sitting down to work on the flan.

She moved around to stand over me looking down while I ate.

"It's an apology," she said. "For Ernesto. For me. Ernesto's been hanging around with some zoot-suit Mexican kids downtown. White soldiers and sailors have been giving them a hard time. This morning he had a run-in with a couple of soldiers before he came home. He came through the door, saw you, and lost his temper."

"And you clobbered me with a soup ladle," I reminded her, touching my slightly swollen jaw.

She leaned over, breathed on my cheek, and touched my sore jaw with warm fingers and just the slightest touch of fingernails.

"I'm sorry," she said. "He's my son, and I was afraid you would hurt him."

I took another bite of the flan.

"Can I taste some of that?" she asked. "I had no time before I came here. I just had time after Ernesto left for work to get dressed and come here."

I spooned up some quivering flan and held it up for her. Her mouth engulfed the spoon and her tongue licked the small sugary spot she had missed. I almost dropped the spoon.

"I'm really sorry about this morning," she whispered, taking the spoon from my hand and putting it on the table.

"Say, listen," I said looking up at her. "I can understand."

"I'd like to make it up to you," she said, touching my hair and my cheek.

I could have told her that the flan and the apology were enough, but I'm no fool, or at least I'm not that big a fool. She leaned over with her mouth open and kissed me, with one hand holding tightly but not pulling my hair. We kissed for a long time, a long drowsy time, before she pulled away slowly.

"Here?" she said.

"No room," I said.

"We'll make room."

She reached over and pushed everything on my desk onto the floor. Old bills, flyers, the last of the flan, a stapler that had been given to me by my ex-wife, a copy of the collected poems of William Blake that Jeremy had given me, and various pencils and paperweights made by my nephews in first and second grade went flying and clattering.

"Enough room?" she said, turning to me with a smile.

"It'll do," I said.

I don't know if you could call what we did making love, but it was definitely engaging in lust. She took the lead, did the undressing, indicated where she wanted me and how, and took over with an experience I didn't want to think about. I came close to that half hour of no-thought I had been seeking.

Was sex meditation? I'd have to ask Jeremy about it some time.

"Relax," she whispered.

"If I relax, we'll never get anywhere," I whispered back.

"It takes care of itself," she said leaning over me on the desk. "You don't have to work at it, just enjoy it."

I did.

When we were finished, or at least when I was finished, she got off the table, went to her purse, and pulled out a cigarette which she lit with no sign of getting dressed. I got up like the somnambulist in *The Cabinet of Dr. Caligari,* tested my back for pain, found none, and rolled off the desk to retrieve my clothes.

Elisa stood at the window naked, smoking, and said,

"There are two men down there fighting."

"They do that a lot," I said. "They just show their teeth. I think they're friends."

"I see," she said.

"You want to get dressed?" I asked, buttoning my shirt.

She turned from the window, grinned, and gave me a moist open-mouthed kiss that got me going again. This time I took off my pants and I didn't get lost in meditation.

When we were finished again, I lay exhausted on the table looking up at the crack in the ceiling that reminded me of the Mississippi River. Elisa got dressed and gathered her things, including the spoon and the now empty bowl, and I sat up without worrying about my back.

"I really enjoyed that," she said, reaching over to touch my cheek.

"I didn't find it agonizing," I answered groggily.

"I didn't kill Lowry," she said.

"But you did know him."

"I . . ." she started.

"I mean you were the one who brought him to the Steistel Brothers," I said, putting on my underwear.

"I met him on another picture," she said. "I knew Miracle

was looking for a Peter Lorre. I suggested Lowry. I'm sorry I did."

"Why?"

"Lowry mistook professional kindness for sexual interest," she said, looking in a mirror and adjusting her makeup. "That became particularly awkward when he brought that Minck woman around."

"What do you know about Lowry?" I asked, considering my shirt and deciding not to put it on.

She kept looking in her mirror, checked her lipstick, shrugged, and said, "German, just came over a year ago. Had a few parts and made a near living selling men's clothing at I. Magnin's on Wilshire. I did not kill him."

"You're not a suspect," I lied.

"Thanks. I believe you," she lied.

We could have gone on lying to each other for a while but the door opened and Jeremy Butler stepped in. Jeremy filled the doorway like a massive walking bomb, the kind that is painted on the fuselages of bombers. His bald head almost reached to top of the door and his nearly 300 pounds almost touched both sides of the doorway.

Elisa stepped back, her heels grinding something she had swept onto the floor.

"Toby," Jeremy said, looking at me nearly undressed on the chair. "Are you all right? Alice told me she let a woman in here."

"Elisa Potter," I said, nodding at Elisa.

"Very pleased to meet you," Jeremy said politely, ignoring the mess and my state of undress.

"Jeremy owns this building," I said. "He's a former wrestler."

Elisa looked at Jeremy with a slightly furrowed brow and then a light of recognition.

"Did you write a book of poetry, *Doves of a Winter Night*?" she asked.

"Yes," Jeremy said.

"God," Elisa said. "I love that book. I got it from a friend."

"Thank you," said Jeremy. The sun was almost gone, but I thought I detected something I never expected to see, Jeremy blushing.

"Oh God, wait till I tell Harold," she said. Before I could wonder who Harold might be, she started to recite:

> Curling over the hills, cloud fingers
> pause to linger
> lovingly against the tips of trees,
> sigh and break free
> like ghosts to roll gently down
> around
> the houses that silent lie
> with windows like open eyes.
> The fog blankets, comforts, hides,
> and then slowly moves back like the tide
> to wait moist-fingered for another evening.

"You have a remarkable memory," said Jeremy, his voice betraying an emotion I'd never heard before.

"I'm an actress," she said. "And I love the poem."

With that she looked at me once, smiled, showing white teeth, touched Jeremy's arm and moved past him through the door, closing it behind her.

"Great exit," I said.

"I . . ." began Jeremy with a loss for words I had never seen before.

"Jeremy, do you think sex can be meditation?" I said, getting out of my chair to get dressed.

"It is located in the wrong chakra," he said, "but . . . it may be possible. Actually, it would be a paradox, a contradiction, but all paradoxes and contradictions are not contradictions at all but an indication that we have set up boundaries that do not exist. So, perhaps sexuality can be a form of meditation."

The last few lines were uttered with Jeremy looking at the closed door through which Elisa had exited. I wondered what Jeremy and Alice's lovemaking must be like. I settled on monumental.

I didn't understand much of what Jeremy said, but it always sounded good when he said it, and it always seemed to make sense. I just couldn't hold on to it.

"Can you hang on a minute, Jeremy? I've got a call to make and then I have something to tell you."

Jeremy indicated that he could wait and began to pick up debris as I called Sal Lurtzma's office. The phone rang and Sal answered.

"Sal, Toby. What does it look like?"

"Like the oversize xylophone I gave my sister's grandson last year," he answered.

"Sal, I'm talking about the Peter Lorre audition."

"The Peter Lorre audition, right," Lurtzma answered and behind him I heard the hollow sound of some instrument. "I thought you meant the marimba. Got a guy here right now, Jose something . . ."

"Econecho," came a voice beyond Sal's.

"That we can change," Sal said. "Anyway, Toby. Guy plays classical marimba but that's not it. He can make the marimba talk, say words. Honest to God, great act. He plays awhile and then stops all of a sudden to have the marimba talk. Give a listen here."

"Sal, will you. . . ?" I tried but Sal was not to be stopped where an act was on the line.

"Make it say hello like before," I heard Sal say somewhere away from the phone. He was probably aiming it toward Jose.

A reverberating trio of notes came over the telephone lines and probably lost something in electrical translation. It didn't sound anything like hello.

"Now," Sal said excitedly in the background, "make it say good-bye."

"Not so easy," came Jose Econecho's voice.

"Life is not easy," said Sal seriously. "But we endure."

More notes on the phone. It didn't sound like a word to me.

"Well?" bubbled Sal coming back on the line. "Did I tell you or did I tell you?"

"You told me, Sal," I said. "It's a miracle. What about the Peter Lorre audition?"

"All taken care of," he said. "Hitching Post Theater tomorrow morning, but it's got to be bright and early. Eight in the morning. You know the Hitching Post?"

"Hollywood and Vine," I said. "Everyone knows the Hitching Post."

The Hitching Post showed only Westerns, old Westerns, new Westerns, any Westerns.

"They got a special for kids Saturday," Sal said. "Triple Don 'Red' Barry bill. They change the posters tomorrow. We've got to be out by ten."

"Ad in the *Times*?" I asked as Jeremy continued to straighten up the place.

"No time, no time," Sal whined. "And no need. I got the word out to all the agents. It's a network. And Jimmy Fiddler's mentioning it tonight. You'll be up to your tuchus in Peter Lorres, Toby. You really think Jose's got something special? Level with me?"

"I never heard a talking marimba act before, Sal. I'm overwhelmed," I said.

"Great, fine. Bring me a check or cash to the audition."

"Remember the *Maine*, Sal," I said and we both hung up. I turned to Jeremy who was standing nearby, having picked up whatever could be picked up.

"Shelly's been kidnaped," I said.

Jeremy, who had been dreaming of Elisa, looked at me.

"To keep me from looking for the person who killed a couple of Peter Lorre impersonators," I explained. "It has something to do with Mildred running away with one of the impersonators."

It was Jeremy's turn to be confused by me.

"I don't follow you, Toby, but I assume you want some assistance from me or you would not have given me news that might needlessly cause distress. It isn't like you."

"Tomorrow morning, eight, at the Hitching Post Theater," I said. "I'm holding tryouts for a Peter Lorre look-alike. It's the real thing. I'm doing it for a company called Miracle Pictures."

"You are also doing it in the hope of drawing a killer," said Jeremy.

"It's that obvious, huh?"

Jeremy shrugged.

"It depends," he said, "on how perceptive your killer is."

"The one I talked to on the phone isn't too perceptive," I said, putting on my shoes.

"Then. . . ?" asked Jeremy.

"Peter Lorre, the real one, is my client. He'll be there. I'd like you to be there and keep an eye on him in case . . ."

"I understand," said Jeremy. "Of course, I'll be there."

"More than that Jeremy," I said. "I'll give him a call and I'd like you to meet him someplace, anyplace, and come to the Hitching Post with him at about a quarter to eight."

"Yes," said Jeremy.

"Yes," I said. "Thanks, Jeremy. I picked up the phone and pulled out my notebook with Sidney Greenstreet's phone number in it. Greenstreet answered it himself after four rings.

"This is Toby Peters," I said.

"Ah, yes, the detective," he said. "Dreadful business. Dreadful. Peter should be more concerned, far more concerned. He is taking this all too lightly."

"I'll try to impress him with the seriousness of the situation," I said soothingly.

"That would be most solicitous of you," said Greenstreet. "He's like a son to me."

"I'll take care of him," I said.

"A son," Greenstreet repeated absently and then, rousing himself from his thoughts. "I'll get him to the phone."

Five minutes later I had the plan worked out with Lorre and Jeremy and was on my way out the door. I had one more stop to make. I felt like Elmer Blurt. I didn't want anyone to be home but I had to make the stop because it was my job.

Twenty minutes later, after listening to the last ten minutes of "People Are Funny" and the first ten of "Lightning Jim," I was parked in front of the Minck house in Inglewood, a house to which I had never been invited because of a head-on dislike Mildred Minck and I had felt toward each other from the moment she first walked into Shelly's office and found that I had set up shop in the broom closet.

After she had made her distaste evident on that first encounter, I had suggested variously and sweetly that she could pass for Shelly's mother, that she could pass for Rondo Hatton's sister, and that it was a pity that able-bodied women couldn't serve in the infantry.

I got out of the car and felt my stomach rumble with hunger. All I'd had in it for more than five hours was two cups of coffee, a slice of baclava, and a dish of flan. There were lights on in the house but I still had hope. I walked to the door, rang the bell, and heard Mildred shout, "Answer the door."

11

Mildred's hulk of a brother, Michael, opened the door and didn't look at all happy to see me. He was wearing a sullen pout and a plaid shirt that he had not tucked into his gray pants. His hair was uncombed and falling into his eyes and he needed a shave.

"What do you want?" he asked through clenched teeth.

"I want to talk to you and Mildred," I said amiably.

"We don't want to talk to you," he said defiantly.

"I didn't think you would," I said. "We haven't exactly been friends and I don't think Mildred remembers me in her prayers every night. This is about murder and about your brother-in-law."

"She threw him out," Lebowitz said, guarding the door.

"Who is it, Michael?" Mildred called irritably from inside. "Stop making that noise. I'm listening to something."

"It's Peters," Michael shouted back.

"He can't come in here," she screeched.

"You can't come in," Lebowitz said, turning to me triumphantly.

Enough is enough. My father used to say that. What he usually meant was that he was at a point where most sensible people would have screamed, rebelled, started throwing things, or given up. But my father was a born victim. When he said "Enough is enough," he usually meant that he was preparing himself for far more than what a sensible person would endure. I don't know what his breaking point was. He never got there. He just died in bed one night when he was sixty-five. However, I am not my father, though I wear his watch. I stepped forward quickly and pushed against the door as hard as I could. The door hit Lebowitz in the shoulder and chin and sent him flying back into the hallway against a closet. I caught the door rebounding toward me, stepped in, and closed it.

Lebowitz pushed himself away from the closet, touched his face, and looked at his hand for blood. There wasn't any.

"What *is* going on out there, Michael?" came Mildred's voice, but she didn't come running to see.

"Get out of here," Lebowitz hissed.

"I want to talk to you and Mildred," I said. "Can I help you?"

I reached out to help him straighten up but he pushed my hands away as if they were attacking snakes.

"I'm calling the police," Lebowitz said, staggering into the living room.

I followed him. It was all Mildred's house. There wasn't a sign of Shelly in it. It was neat, white, clean. The furniture was covered with clear material that made it plain no one was to sit on it. The lamps were polished steel and the pictures on the wall modern, colorful, and representing nothing I recognized. On top of a white endtable sat a fat, white porcelain Buddha. I was sure the rest of the house was as unlived in as this room.

Lebowitz reached for the phone on another white endtable.

"Ask for Lieutenant Seidman at the Wilshire district station," I advised, looking for something halfway comfortable to sit on and finding nothing. "I'll just have a seat and wait."

Lebowitz bounced the phone in his hand and glared at me.

Deeper in the small house, a door opened and Irene Rich's voice came sweetly over the radio saying, "Dear John, today I . . ."

"What is going on, Michael?" Mildred bleated. "I'm trying to listen to my show."

"Mike," I said, "either call the cops, answer your sister, answer my questions, or try to throw me out."

Lebowitz put down the phone and stepped back toward me.

"I could tear you in half, Peters," he said looking down at me.

He hadn't gotten any smaller since I had last seen him, but he hadn't gotten any braver either.

"Problem is, Mike, you'd have to fight to find out and we both know you don't have the heart for it," I said gently. "The time to throw me out was before you moved for the phone. You went for help. Get your sister in here."

Before he could spit something out Mildred came stomping into the living room. Her hair was up and shiny as if it had been glued in place. She wore a pink robe that did not flatter her. It would have taken a high-priced escort from La Douce Escort Service on Pico to flatter Mildred. The radio had either been turned off or down or she had closed a door before billowing out to the living room.

"Peters, you get out. Get out of here," she said, pointing at the door in case I didn't know where to find it and might consider a mad rush through the locked windows. "Michael, throw him out of here."

"We've been through that, Mildred," I said. "Michael isn't throwing anybody out and he's not calling the police. Sheldon's been kidnaped."

She stopped, open-mouthed, her hand still pointing toward the door.

"I'll call the police," Michael announced. "Milly, I'll call the police."

"Shut up and sit down, Michael," Mildred said, her face pale. "But not in here. This room is for guests."

She gulped and her hand came down to her side. I wondered what guests merited sitting on this immaculate, uncomfortable furniture.

"Let's go into the kitchen," she said, and closed her pink robe around her with a shudder.

"After you," I said, and she led the way down a short corridor and to the left into a metal kitchen. The chairs had metal legs and seats made out of the same green, artificial material as the top of the table, which also had metal legs. The whole room was green and metallic, including the refrigerator and the cabinets. No food was showing. Everything was behind closed doors and the place looked as if it had just been completed for a window display.

"Cozy," I said, pulling out a chair that squealed over the shiny green and white linoleum floor. I sat and looked up at Mildred.

Michael hovered over another kitchen chair, unsure of what to do. I had the feeling that, in Shelly's absence, little brother was playing a role he had escaped from long ago, and found himself falling into with horror and a desire to run.

"Sit down, Michael," Mildred commanded, hugging herself. Michael sat. "Now," she went on looking at me. "What's this about Sheldon being kidnaped? No one has contacted me about ransom. I think this is one of Sheldon's tricks to win me back. Actually, I think it's one of your tricks, and you've put him up to it."

"No trick," I said. "I'm the one against the wall, not you. Whoever took him wants me to stop looking for your boyfriend's killer."

"No one asked you to look for Peter's killer," she said with tears starting in the corners of her eyes. Her voice was something between the death sound of a dying grackle and static on the Blue Network.

"The real Peter Lorre is paying me," I said. "And whoever killed your friend used my gun. I'm still a suspect. Shouldn't we be worrying about your husband here?"

"We'll call the police," she said. "I still don't believe you, but we'll just call the police. I still think you killed Peter. Sheldon didn't want me to have my freedom, and he paid you to kill my lover. There, I said it. I'm glad I said it. Michael will call the police."

"Me?" cried Michael. "Why me? He's your husband."

"I've already told the police," I said.

"Then what do you want?" croaked Mildred. "Peter is dead. It's all over."

"Sheldon, your husband," I reminded her. "I'd really like to get him back alive. Maybe you can tell me something about Lowry that will help, like who Steinholtz might be."

"He never mentioned any Steinholtz," she said, pulling out a chair and sitting on it. "Michael, I need Kleenex."

Michael jumped up as if he'd sat on a Whoopie Cushion and hurried across the room.

"And tuck in your shirt, Michael," she yelled after him.

"Lowry," I reminded her when Michael was gone.

"He lied to me. He deceived me. I've always been lied to and deceived by men. I thought he was Peter Lorre. I really did. He told me he was. He seemed so . . . right. Even after I found out I couldn't give him up and go back to Sheldon. You, even you, can see that."

"I see that you could have killed him," I said. "You or your weasel brother. You felt deceived. You wanted revenge. You've got a temper and a weak brother."

Michael came scurrying back into the room, Kleenex in hand. He handed them to Mildred, who looked at his shirt. Michael quickly tucked it in. I didn't think I saw a murderer in the kitchen, but you never know till the final bell rings.

"What did you know about Lowry?" I said. "Relatives? Anything? Where did he live?"

"He was currently traveling," Mildred said touching her nose with a tissue. "He had a room in the Ravenswood on Rossmore in Hollywood, a very nice room."

"What number?" I asked.

"Seven oh four," Mildred said. "I've already told the police everything, everything. I bared my soul to them, to that zombie of a detective who never smiled or showed the slightest warmth."

"Lieutenant Seidman," I said. "He's a sweetheart."

"I don't want Sheldon to be killed," Mildred announced, crumpling her Kleenex in her palm and folding her white-knuckled hands on the green table top.

"I'm sure that will make him happy if I can get the news to him," I said.

"I don't want him killed," she said, "but I can no longer live with him, not now that I've tasted life for the first time. I'm still a woman with needs. I want to live."

It sounded like a bad Norma Shearer imitation to me, but I wasn't going to argue with her. The way I figured it, taking into account my vast experience as a marriage counselor, Shelly would be better off without her, but I could be wrong. I'd been wrong once or twice an hour most of my life.

"I can understand that," I said. "Did Lowry say anything the day he died? Anything that showed he was upset, excited?"

"Nothing," Mildred said.

"He was happy," said Michael.

"Well, yes," said Mildred, "but that was because we had reconciled our differences."

"He said he was going to make some money," Michael said.

"How?" I asked Michael who seemed to have run out of information and sank down in his uncomfortable chair with a shrug. Mildred mustered a disapproving glare and Michael sat up and ran a hand over his hair.

"I don't know," Mildred answered with a sob. "It happened so suddenly. In the morning he had been cold, distant, upset that I wouldn't give him . . ." She hesitated.

I guessed at what she wouldn't give him and I was sure it wasn't sex.

". . . money," I said.

"Yes," she said, holding her head up to show her red eyes.

"And before the Steistels started to shoot the scene on the roof Lowry got happy and said he was coming into money?" I asked.

"Yes," she said.

"And the money was coming from?" I coaxed.

"Someone. I don't really care. It's all over," she wailed, putting her head down on her clenched fists.

Michael reached over to comfort her and then pulled his hand back as it was about to touch Mildred's finely lacquered hair. He looked at me for a suggestion. I had none for him.

"Thanks," I said, getting up.

Michael looked at me and Mildred with sudden fear.

"You want some coffee?" he asked pleadingly. He didn't want to be left alone with his sister, but I wasn't in the business of rescuing cowardly brothers.

"Sorry," I said moving toward the kitchen door. "I've got a dentist to save."

Mildred sobbed, choked, and said, "Michael, turn on the radio, KNX."

Michael jumped up, moved to the white-curtained kitchen window, and turned on the little white Philco. He fiddled with the dial and I walked out without waiting for good-byes. In the living room I grabbed the Buddha.

When I hit the front door, I heard the voice of an announcer say, "And the makers of Welch's Grape Juice invite you to join Irene Rich at our new time and new network for the next letter to Dear John."

"Over," wailed Mildred. "It's all over."

I went through the front door wondering if she was talking about her radio show, her marriage, her moment of passion with Lowry, or her husband's life.

There was one more piece of business before I closed the shop, turned off the lights, and went home to the bosom of my family in Kansas City, Kansas. I found a phone booth next to a gas station, called Hollywood 5391 and asked for the house detective. The Ravenswood was a little above most of the places where I knew the house man, but in this case I was lucky. Higby was a cop when I was a cop back in Glendale. Higby retired and went to work at the Ravenswood, complete with an assistant. I went to work for Warner Brothers as a security guard till Harry Warner took a dislike to me when, as I've mentioned, I punched a Warner B movie cowboy star in the mouth when I was supposed to be guarding him.

"Higby," came Higby's voice, slightly high-pitched, deceptively bubbly.

"George, it's Toby Peters," I said.

"Toby . . . God almightly, it's been five years," he said.

"More like six or seven," I said. "How're the halls of the Ravenswood?"

"Mostly quiet," he said. "What comes up I manage to put down. How you going?"

"Private investigation. What comes up I patch up."

"I hear Phil made captain?" Higby said.

"Early this year," I said.

"How's Anne?" he went on.

"We're divorced, but we keep in touch. She's fine, visiting her sister back in Ohio. Her second husband died last year," I said hoping he didn't ask for details. "How's . . ."

"Amelia," he supplied. "Fine, kids are fine. We hang up now or you tell me what this is about?"

"Guy registered in the Ravenswood got himself killed the other day," I said.

"Kindem, also known as Pete R. Lowry," Higby said. "Cops have already checked his room. You on the case?"

"I'm on it for a client. Think I could take a look at Lowry's room?"

"Lieutenant named Seidman's already been through it," said Higby. "Seemed to know what he was doing."

"Right, he does," I said. "But I might be looking for something that didn't mean anything to Seidman. I've been on the thing for a couple of days and have some leads."

"And someone to protect?"

"Just the body, not the reputation, George. You can stand at my side to be sure I don't walk off with the candlesticks and telephones. Give me twenty minutes."

A pause, a sigh, and then,

"If you get here in less than an hour, I'll give you ten minutes in his room. No relatives have shown up and I can't see how it can hurt him."

"Thanks, George," I said.

"Thanks comes in all shapes, sizes, and denominations," said Higby.

"Ten bucks and my thanks," I said.

"Fifteen and your respect," he answered.

"See you in twenty minutes."

About eighteen minutes later, after catching Billie Holiday singing the blues on her KFWB show, I found a parking space next to the garden to the right of the Ravenswood. Finding Higby was no problem. He was waiting at the entrance, hands in pockets, tie loose, stomach trying to escape from the shirt about a size too small. He looked older than I remembered him, which shouldn't have been a surprise.

"George."

"Toby."

We shook hands and I handed him three fives, which he jammed into his pocket. The rest was pure business and small talk about the old days. We went up to Lowry's room where he opened the door with a passkey and while I searched we talked about the old days, who was alive, who was in the army, who had retired, and who were our favorite bad guys. His favorites were the steady regulars, the repeat housebreakers, car thieves. My favorites were the crazies, not because I was fond of them but because they gave me nightmares. Being with Higby reminded me of the woman with the broken pool cue who skewered her husband and took off after me when my partner and I came in answer to the neighbors' calls. My partner had to break her arm to stop her because she thought I was the incarnation of her husband, who lay dead in the kitchen. She was one of my favorite crazies. Then there was the machine-gun kid, a fifteen-year-old who taped four of his father's rifles together, rigged a strip of inner tube to the triggers and filled my squad car and my partner full of holes. When I got the kid cuffed he claimed that it wasn't his idea, that John Gilbert had come to him in a dream and given him the idea for the homemade machine gun and Gilbert who told him to shoot at the first passing police car. My partner lived and three years later when I checked on the kid in the state mental hospital he was writing long letters to John Gilbert asking the actor to come forward and tell the truth or he would have to get out and punish him.

Those were the kind that haunted me, the ones you couldn't figure. I was about to remind Higby of Alphonse the Needler when I found something interesting in the drawer of the desk near the window. The room had been easy to go through, not too much clothing, only a few pictures of Lowry doing his best to look like Peter Lorre, some magazines, and an old leather suitcase in good shape in the closet. But in the desk was an envelope and in the envelope were photographs. There weren't many of them and they were all family-type pictures, chubby mom looking awkwardly at the camera, stern father with a beard holding his hat under his arm, a pair of boys, one of whom was probably Lowry. My favorite was a shot of Lowry holding a tennis racket and kneeling, his eyes toward the camera. Kneeling at his side was the real Peter Lorre, also holding a tennis racket and smiling. Standing between them was a man who couldn't be identified because the top half of the picture had been torn off.

"Steinholtz," I said, looking through the envelope and drawer for the top half of the photograph. I didn't find it.

"Don't remember him," said Higby who was fiddling with a brass letter opener in the shape of a scimitar. "Was he a cop or a crazy?"

"A crazy," I said.

"What was the story on Steinholtz?" Higby asked as I slid the photograph into my side pocket.

"It's not over. When it is I'll let you know. I think I've seen enough."

"Suit yourself, Toby," said Higby. "Got time for a cup of java? On me. I've got all night."

"No thanks, George," I said. "I've got some work to do."

"The curse of the self-employed," sighed Higby. "You make yourself work hours you'd quit over in a regular job."

I agreed, told him the story of Alphonse the Needler which, I was pleased to see, made him shudder, and left the Ravenswood after some handshakes and lies about getting together soon.

I drove to Levy's on Spring, remembering Elisa and looking forward to Saturday night and Carmen, but Carmen had already left for the night. I didn't eat. I was tired and had to get up early for the Lorre audition, so I headed for home.

Parking on Heliotrope was no problem. I had no real hope of getting past Mrs. Plaut so I didn't try tiptoeing, didn't take off my shoes. She was sitting in the doorway of her room when I came through the front door with Shelly's Buddha under my arm. She was sitting with a rectangular brown package on her lap.

"Mr. Peelers," she said, "I have been waiting for you."

She looked at me as if I should have something to tell her but I didn't.

"Mr. Peelers," she went on, getting no satisfaction or help from me. "Marie Dressler has been shot."

"Marie Dressler?" I said stunned.

"This morning on the very porch you have just traversed," she said.

"On your porch? This morning?"

With this she opened the package in her lap and pulled out the photograph of Eleanor Roosevelt that had been hit that morning when Lowry's killer had taken a shot at me. The glass was cracked and the hole clear. To emphasize the reality of the situation, Mrs. Plaut put her small finger through the bullet hole.

"It went right through," she said, shaking her head.

"It would have been a miracle if it had stopped half way," I said.

"Who would want to shoot Marie Dressler?" Mrs. Plaut asked, perplexed.

"Eleanor Roosevelt," I said.

"Eleanor Roosevelt would want to shoot Marie Dressler?" Mrs. Plaut asked, looking up at me with eyes wide.

"No, the photograph is of Eleanor Roosevelt, not Marie Dressler," I explained.

Mrs. Plaut looked at the photo again as if she had never seen it before.

"A remarkable resemblance," she said.

"Remarkable," I agreed, though I didn't think the two women looked at all alike. I also agreed because I wasn't sure what Mrs. Plaut found remarkable. Did she still think the photo was Marie Dressler who looked like Eleanor Roosevelt, or did she think it was Eleanor Roosevelt who bore a remarkable resemblance to Marie Dressler?

"But why would anyone want to shoot her? Republicans don't drive down Heliotrope," she said, looking deeply into Eleanor Roosevelt's eyes.

"They were shooting at me," I said.

She looked up and adjusted her hearing aid.

"At me," I repeated.

"I see," said Mrs. Plaut with relief. "Thank the Lord."

"Right," I said. "Just me, not a photograph."

"You can't know what a relief that is," she said, putting her tiny right hand on the place where her heart was supposed to be beneath her blue dress. "I'll get the photograph repaired and put right back where it was with confidence that it will not happen again."

"I'm going to bed, Mrs. Plaut," I sighed, heading up the stairs.

"I have a list of people we must visit tomorrow," she called after me, her spirits returned.

"People. . . ?"

"Rubber, Mr. Peelers, rubber. We must urge our neighbors to check their garages, attics. We must, according to Joseph F. MacCaughtry, who the president has named to head the general salvage campaign, double our efforts for our boys overseas."

"Sunday, Mrs. Plaut, Sunday. I can't tomorrow. I'm working tomorrow and Saturday," I said.

"Then Sunday," she said, "but remember you might be keeping vital caches of rubber from our boys overseas. A delay of two days might mean lives."

"I'll have to live with that responsibility, Mrs. Plaut," I said and hurried up the rest of the stairs and down the hall to Gunther's room. I listened before I knocked. Behind his door I could hear music. I knocked and Gunther called, "Come in."

Gunther Wherthman's room was a display of efficiency. In one corner was a work space, complete with desk and a row of bookcases filled with texts. A folding seven-panel oak divider decorated with scenes of Geneva separated the work space from the sleeping and rest space where Gunther's neatly made bed stood. Across from the bed was an old brown chair, not too stuffed, complete with ottoman and, to the right, separated from both spaces was the kitchen area, neatly arranged with table, two chairs, and matching pewter salt and pepper shakers.

Gunther was seated at his desk working in longhand while he listened to one of his Bach records. He had taken off the jacket of the three-piece suit he'd worn that day and had put on a blue robe. Gunther would not take off his suit till bedtime. He glanced over his left shoulder at me as I entered, removed his glasses, and turned down the volume on the machine.

"Bach," I said.

"You are developing an appreciation?" Gunther asked, getting down from the chair.

"I don't know. Maybe. You always play Bach."

"Not always," he said. "There is Mozart, Vivaldi, and the Italian operas."

"Maybe I am developing something," I said.

"Do not be afraid of good taste, Toby," he said, moving toward the kitchen area. "It will not tarnish your image in the eyes of your friends. Coffee?"

"No thanks, Gunther, I've got to get some sleep. I'm going to eat something and go to bed. What's tomorrow like for you?"

Gunther nodded his small head toward his desk.

"I've got some work to do bright and early, and I could use your help," I went on.

"It involves Peter Lorre?" he asked.

"Yeah."

"I will be most pleased to render assistance," he said. "Tell me where to be and what I must do."

I told him what to do. He stood with his tiny hands in the pocket of his robe, listened, and made a few suggestions that made sense to me.

"See you in the morning, Gunther," I said.

"Wait," he called and hurried to his refrigerator. He pulled out a plate covered with foil and brought it over to me. "A pâté," he explained. "My own recipe."

"Thanks," I said. "I'll eat it and get to bed."

Back in my room, I turned on the light, took off my jacket, put Shelly's Buddha and his glasses on my dresser, and went to my kitchen table. I didn't pause to compare my room to Gunther's.

If it weren't for Mrs. Plaut's frequent intrusions, I'd need Frank Buck to lead a safari through the mess. I found a few not-too-stale slices of Wonder Bread, dropped Gunther's pate on one of them and smeared a healthy glob of mayo on the other. I ate the sandwich, washing it down with a half-full bottle of milk. It wasn't bad but the sandwich wasn't enough. I had some milk left, so I got down the oversized Terry and the Pirates bowl my nephews had given me for my birthday, emptied the last of my Puffed Rice and Shredded Ralston into it, and poured on the rest of the milk. I ate slowly, going over my plan for the next morning. It wasn't much of a plan, but I had a full stomach and the memory of Elisa in my office. I also had a client and enough money to buy cereal and milk and pay for my room.

I laid out my clothes for the morning, pulled the mattress off the bed onto the floor as I did every night, turned off the lights, and fell asleep listening to the faint sound of Gunther's Bach records through the wall.

If I were right, I'd have Shelly free and a killer nailed within forty-eight hours. If I were wrong, I could get a few people killed, including me. It could have been worse. I could have been young enough to get drafted.

12

Morning came with a knock on the door and the last fragment of a dream. The dream had something to do with Elisa Morales or Potter and the photograph I'd found in Lowry's room at the Ravenswood. I had a sense that I had tried Elisa's head on the body in the photograph but it didn't fit. I wondered as I sat up if I had tried the heads of the rest of the people involved.

"What, what?" I called looking up blearily at my Beech-Nut gum clock.

The early Friday morning sunlight caught the glass covering the clock face. I rolled to the side to see the time. Six-fifteen.

"Toby?" called Gunther. "It is time."

"Come in," I said, chewing on the morning grit in my dry mouth.

Gunther entered, elegantly garbed with a small white fedora and carrying a half-sized cane.

"You look spiffy, Gunther," I said sitting up and scratching my stomach through my undershirt.

"Thank you," he said.

"You have a sword in that cane?" I asked. "Or is it a one-shot rifle?"

Gunther examined his cane without a smile and answered, "It is simply a cane, which I believe is appropriate for this weather. Do you find it somehow threatening or sinister? That was not at all my intent."

"Forget it, Gunther," I said, biting my lower lip and feeling the stubble of overnight against my teeth. "I'm still waking up."

Gunther checked his pocket watch and suggested that I had best hurry and that the washroom was empty and would probably remain so till Mr. Hill the mailman got up at six-thirty.

"Now, you know what to do?" I asked.

Gunther looked slightly offended.

"I'm sorry," I apologized. "I'm counting on you."

"And I shall not fail you," he said. "But please, Toby, exercise caution, as will I."

"I will, Gunther. See you later," I said.

Gunther left and I got up after testing my back. I worked my jaw and found the spot where Elisa had ladled me. It wasn't too bad. My various other vulnerable spots didn't scream out as I adjusted my underwear, grabbed my toothpaste, a not-too-dirty towel, and razor and staggered out of my room toward the washroom.

The shower was warm, not hot, and it came out in a reluctant trickle rather than a spray, but it was enough. I washed, shaved, and sang the Wildroot Cream Oil song. When I got out of the tub, I cleared the mirror over the sink and brushed my teeth. The face in front of me still looked tough, but I thought I saw a softness in the brown eyes that I didn't like. It wasn't that I denied that softness. I just didn't like the idea that it showed. I made some tough faces in the mirror. I tried Barton MacLane, Jack LaRue, Jack Dempsey, and Henry Armstrong but I couldn't convince myself. I settled for Max Baer.

The phone on the landing was ringing when I stepped into the hall with the towel draped around me and a handful of toiletries. I padded barefoot to get it before it woke anyone up who didn't have to be up.

"Hello," I said. "This is Mrs. Plaut's boardinghouse. Can I help you?"

"Peters?"

"Yes," I said, recognizing the Mickey Mouse voice from the day before.

"You didn't stop," he said.

"I told you I wouldn't. Hey, I've got to get dressed. I've got somewhere to be in less than two hours. I haven't got time for you."

"We'll kill the dentist. I swear we will," the caller said, trying to be calm.

"No, you won't," I said. "Look, I've really got to go. If I don't have some clean socks, I'm going to have to rinse the ones I've got on and I'm not sure I can dry them on my hot plate in time. But I am glad you called. I found a photograph of Steinholtz in Lowry's apartment."

"You're bluffing," the caller said, frightened. "We tore the head off of that picture."

"You're right," I said, grinning because he had confirmed that the photograph was Steinholtz. "I'm bluffing. You have any more information for me? How about putting Minck on the phone?"

"He won't wake up," Mickey Mouse whined. "And he snores. I had to spend the night here with him and I didn't get any sleep. He talks and talks and talks. You know what he talks about?"

"Teeth," I said.

"Teeth," the kidnaper confirmed. "In his sleep, he says crazy things about teeth, people with missing teeth, fake teeth. He's driving me nuts."

"Let him go," I said. "I'm going to catch you soon anyway."

"No, you're not," he cried.

"Hey, I'm in a good mood and you're ruining my morning. You like cereal?"

"Cereal?"

"Yeah, cereal," I said. "Helps me get to sleep at night and start the morning. I'm going to borrow some milk and have some Wheaties. Try it. It might make you feel better."

"Peters," he shouted.

"Quiet," I said. "You'll wake Shelly. Good-bye."

I hung up. So far my strategy of dealing with the kidnapers

seemed to be working. I tried not to think about whether I'd have enough nerve to try the same thing if they had taken Gunther or Anne or Mrs. Plaut. I knew there was no chance of their taking Jeremy. They had probably taken the wrong hostage, but it wasn't the first mistake they'd made.

I had half a small bottle of cream I had planned to use for coffee. I dumped it on a bowl of Wheaties and drank the coffee straight without sugar. I had no sugar left. Mrs. Plaut had confiscated my sugar ration book and I had half a month to go till I got a new booklet of stamps.

After I put the dishes in the sink, rinsed them, and straightened the room, which meant putting the mattress back on the bed and throwing the blanket more or less evenly over it, I put together enough pieces of clothing to look respectable. No one could tell the difference between a navy blue sock and a black one unless they bent down and looked. The brown slacks were close to clean and reasonably unwrinkled. The white shirt had all the buttons and the frays in the collar were in the back where they couldn't be seen unless you were the kind of person who looked at people's socks and collars. The pants almost matched the orange and blue tie a former client who now taught at the University of Illinois had sent me. The jacket was blue, tweed, too heavy for the weather, and maybe dark enough to pass in a badly lit theater. It was the best I could do and better than I usually did. I put Shelly's glasses in my pocket, tucked his Buddha under my arm, and went out to meet the day and Mrs. Plaut.

She was on the porch in her gray dress and pink sweater. She sat on the porch swing clutching the photograph of Eleanor Roosevelt in her arms.

"Mr. Gunther informed me that you were rising to greet the dawn," she said. "Were it anyone but Mr. Gunther I would have cast doubts, but he's a reliable little gentleman, much like my late mister."

"He is that," I said. "I've got to go catch a killer, Mrs. Plaut." I looked at my father's watch but didn't bother to check the time to see how many hours off it might be.

"You can drop me on Alvarado in front of Mr. Cannon's shop," she went on, getting out of the swing. "He will repair Marie Dressler. Recall, Marie Dressler would not be in need of repair if someone had not shot at you."

It was a small enough price to pay. I wondered if Mr. Cannon opened his shop at seven in the morning but I didn't ask.

"I shall walk back from Mr. Cannon's," she announced, walking ahead of me down the white wooden steps.

On the drive, Mrs. Plaut, clutching her beloved photograph, filled me in on the scrap rubber situation.

"One cent per pound will be paid for rubber," she said. "And the rubber can be turned in at the service station. It will then be shipped to Akron, Ohio, where it will be reclaimed."

"That's nice," I said.

"This automobile is very small," she observed, squirming.

"It saves gas and rubber," I said.

"Grease will be collected starting late in June," she went on, looking through the front window toward that wonderful June day. "Grease and fat for a penny a pound. We shall keep our empty tin cans and fill them. It's the glycerin in the fats."

"The glycerin," I said politely, reaching over to turn on the radio. She turned it off before it could hum into action.

"Glycerin, which can be refined into nitroglycerin," she explained. "I've already volunteered our services, yours and mine."

"I'm honored, Mrs. Plaut," I said.

"We will go door to door and have insignias I can sew onto our jackets very like the ones the air-raid wardens wear," she said.

"Do we get tin hats like the civil defense workers?" I asked.

"That," she said as I pulled over in front of Cannon's on Alvarado, "would be pointless. In case of an air raid, we will stop collecting grease and do our best to find shelter."

When she got out, I turned on the radio, listened to confirmation that the Japanese had landed in the Aleutians and the news that General Tinker had died in the Battle of Midway. I turned off the radio and headed up Hollywood, past Grauman's and around the corner on Vine where I found a parking space without too much trouble. It was a little after seven and the people who prowled the area weren't up yet except for the usual stray sailors who never seemed to know where to go or what to do.

There was already a line in front of the Hitching Post, about twenty-five men. The line was a little ragged. They didn't know the rules here but they had been to auditions before. Some of them were talking in clusters. Many of them were smoking. Some of them even looked a little like Peter Lorre. I moved through them and tried the doors. Since I didn't look like a Peter Lorre imitator, one of the waiting men near the door said, "You know anything about this job?"

"It's straight," I said. "I'm doing the hiring."

"What does it pay?" he said.

I looked at him and decided he was no double for the dead Lowry or Peter Lorre. He was too big, too heavy, and his eyes were too small.

"Not much," I said.

"That's more than I've got, buddy," he said.

I knocked at the glass door of the Hitching Post again and something moved in the lobby. A pair of figures moved toward me out of the darkness near the popcorn and candy stand. One of them was Fat Sal Lurtzma. The other guy was about Sal's age, with a sagging, sad hound face. They opened the door and I walked in.

"Toby, this is Wayne. Wayne is responsible. Wayne, this is Toby," said Sal. "Toby, give me the fifty. Give Wayne ten and I'm on my way. I'm not used to getting up this early. It was in the L.A. *Times* this morning and Jimmy Fiddler mentioned it last night. I got the word out. Even Millman is sending some people over."

"You did fine, Sal," I said, "but I haven't got the cash."

"Cash," Wayne insisted with his mouth almost closed.

"What?" I said.

"He said 'cash,'" Sal answered, rubbing the mop of hair on his head nervously. "Wayne used to be a ventriloquist, damned good too. I handled him. Don't handle ventriloquists anymore though. Now Wayne does some theater managing. I told him ten, Toby."

"You didn't tell me, Sal," I said, fishing out my wallet and handing Wayne two fives, which left me four singles.

"Thanks," said Wayne, pocketing the money. "I'll get the lights on."

Wayne walked away and Sal whispered, "He was funny but a lousy ventriloquist, lousy."

"I can see he was funny," I said.

"Fifty dollars cash," Sal said. "I got a tip on the first race at Aqueduct. Sturdy Duck on top with Mervyn LeRoy to place or show."

"Mervyn LeRoy's a director," I said.

"And a horse," he said. "Don't change the subject. Fifty bucks. Cash on the line or the deal's off and there are Peter Lorres lining up out there."

I looked out the glass windows. The number of Peter Lorres had doubled in the few minutes I'd been inside smelling last night's popcorn and talking to Sal. One of the Lorres, however, was advancing to the door with Jeremy Butler right beside him. I hurried over to open the door and let them in.

"I'm sorry we are a bit late," Lorre apologized, "but I prevailed upon Mr. Butler to have a bit of breakfast. Mr. Butler is a remarkable gentleman."

Lorre was dressed completely in black, black shoes, pants, jacket, and knit shirt with no tie. Jeremy wore dark slacks and a loose gray sweater.

"Mr. Lorre," Sal Lurtzma oozed, stepping forward to take the actor's right hand. "I'm Sal Lurtzma, the agent. We met before, at a fund-raiser for Chinese orphans at the Beverly."

"Pleased to meet you again, Mr. Lurtzma," Lorre said with an amiable smile. "I remember the charming lady you were with."

"We're not together anymore," Sal said, almost crying. "It's a long story, a sad story worthy of a film."

"Not now, Sal," I said, and then to Lorre, "Have you got fifty bucks with you? Sal wants his fee for setting this up."

"I can wait," said Sal, pulling his hands back as if the idea of accepting money from Peter Lorre was unthinkable.

"Nonsense," said Lorre, pulling out his wallet and counting five tens. "You deserve immediate payment and our thanks."

Sal took the money without counting it, shifted it to his left hand, and took Lorre's right again.

"Listen, if you're ever in need of representation," Sal whispered, a line of sweat forming on his upper lip, "remember the name of Sal Lurtzma."

Lorre grasped Sal's hand in both his hands and whispered back, "I shall not forget."

Lurtzma let go, looked at me and Jeremy triumphantly, and walked out the door of the Hitching Post.

"You really remember Sal from some charity thing at the Beverly?" I asked.

"Of course not," sighed Lorre. "But it is always safe to refer to a charming lady. It is flattering whether true or not. Seldom will a man deny to himself or to you that he might have been in the company of a charming woman or at least one that someone found charming."

"I'll try to remember that," I said. "Jeremy told you . . ."

"Yes," said Lorre. "He informed me quite clearly."

Jeremy, who had placed himself between Lorre and the glass doors, nodded and said, "I suggest we move away from these glass doors into a more protected area. It is one thing to accept our fate and quite another to tempt it."

"But," said Lorre, surreptitiously pulling out a silver case and removing a cigarette, "if our fate is written then we cannot tempt it, only fruitlessly seek to avoid it, in which case we become a source of amusement for the gods."

"But," Jeremy said solemnly, "as Schopenhauer said, 'We must live and act as if we have a choice, a control over our futures, or we will simply sit in the corner and wait for death.'"

"Or," said Lorre blowing out a puff of smoke, "enter into a state of meditation like certain Buddhist priests who attain the blissful state of Nirvana."

"Hey, guys," I said. "This is great, fascinating, but until that great come-and-get-it day, I'd like to keep my client alive, save a dentist, and eat regular. Let's get this going."

"As you wish," said Lorre.

We moved through the lobby, past the decor of saddles and horses, past the posters of Buck Jones, Colonel Tim McCoy, Hoot Gibson, Tom Tyler, Kermit and Ken Maynard, Wild Bill Elliott, Gene Autry, Roy Rogers and Tex Ritter. The lights had been turned on in the theater and we walked up the aisle and climbed the steps to the stage.

"Before we start," I said. "Take a look at this."

I pulled the photograph I'd taken from Lowry's desk out of my jacket pocket and handed it to Lorre. His eyes opened with interest.

"This was taken many years ago in Vienna," he said. "I was doing *Faust* with the Vienna repertory company. That would be 1925 or '26. Where did you get this?"

"In the hotel room of that man," I said, pointing at Lowry in the picture. "That's the man who got killed on Wednesday morning, the one who was doing an imitation of you."

"Klausfueler," Lorre muttered.

"What does that mean?" I asked.

"Mean? No, that was his name, Ernst Klausfueler. He was a second cousin," Lorre explained, trying to hand the picture back to me. I pushed it back toward him. "I haven't seen him in more than fifteen years."

"Here he used the names Kindem or Lowry," I said.

"A man of many names," Lorre said. "Not uncommon in our profession. Lorre is not, as you know, my name. Klausfueler understudied me a bit and did nonspeaking roles because of the superficial family resemblance. He really wasn't very good. I never really liked him."

"The other man," I said.

Lorre looked at the photograph.

"His head is missing," Lorre said.

"His name is Steinholtz," I said. "Klausfueler or Kindem or Lowry said his name just before he died. I think Steinholtz killed Lowry and maybe wants to kill you."

Lorre looked at the photograph again.

"The name is vaguely familiar," he said, furrowing his brow.

"Maybe if you saw him again you could put a face to that body," I said.

"Perhaps," Lorre said. "Steinholtz. It . . . I remember. Yes, of course. Steinholtz. He was a brownshirt."

"A Nazi," I said.

"Yes," said Lorre. "He hung around the theater, but there was something about him. I think he was not very highly regarded by his fellow Nazis. He appeared to be embarrassed by their antisemitism. At least that is what I recall about him. I only knew him a short time and then he disappeared. There were rumors that he had been thrown out of the Nazi party by Hitler himself, but we heard so many stories . . ."

"Can I let them in?" called Wayne from the back of the theater. "We got to get this rolling. We got Don 'Red' Barry coming in at eleven and the kids'll start lining up by ten or ten-thirty."

"Let them in," I said, and Wayne walked through the doors at the rear of the theater while I told Lorre to sit offstage with Jeremy where he couldn't be seen.

"If you see Steinholtz or anyone who could be Steinholtz, tell Jeremy. He may not be coming up to audition but he might be sitting in the audience looking for you."

Lorre and Jeremy moved into the darkness to the left of the stage and I stood in front of the curtain as a horde of Peter Lorres swept into the theater.

"Sit anywhere," I shouted. "Anywhere. You'll all get a chance."

Wayne came back when the fifty or so Lorres were seated and looked up at me, trying to catch my eye. Some of them looked pretty good. Others looked nothing like Lorre, but had a look of threat or despair in their eyes.

"You want me to give out numbers?" Wayne called.

"Numbers, right," I said.

"Want me to shuffle them up?" Wayne called.

"Of course," I said. "Shuffle them."

Wayne had the numbers ready. He marched down the aisle passing them out. Peter Lorres groaned, laughed, muttered, sighed when they took their pieces of paper and I made a mental note to give Wayne a bonus with Lorre's money.

"What is this job?" came a voice from the audience.

"Movie," I said. "Finishing a movie. The lead died."

"Peter Lorre died?" came another voice, which sent a murmur through the hall.

"No, a guy named Lowry died. Low budget movie. He was doing a Peter Lorre imitation in the movie," I said.

"What studio and what does it pay?" came another voice.

"Pays five hundred for a week of work and you get costar billing. Miracle Pictures," I announced.

"Miracle?" groaned two or three voices familiar with the company.

About ten or twelve Lorres got up and were headed for the door.

"Hold it. Wait," I called. "You can go if you like but I want to ask you something first. All of you. Has anything happened to you in the last week, any of you? I mean any accident, anything like that?"

The departers hesitated and the actors all looked around at each other.

"In addition to Lowry, another Lorre imitator was killed yesterday, a third got shot at, and a fourth had a minor accident that might not have been an accident," I said.

"What?" a voice came incredulously.

"No joke," I shouted. "Just think."

"Someone pushed me in front of a car a few days ago," came a voice.

"A display of Coke cases almost fell on me in Ralph's this morning," came another voice.

A third man stood up and claimed that a shot had been taken at him.

A fourth and fifth got up, shouting that bombs had been placed in their cars.

All over the theater, Lorres were standing up to give testimony of attempts on their lives. Within three minutes there were so many reports that if half of them were true it would have required the cooperation of the entire First Army in a massive conspiracy. There was no way to separate the real attempts, if there were any, from the invented ones, which there surely were.

"OK. OK. Forget it," I said. "Just a warm-up to get you all loose. Forget the whole thing. Let's get on with the audition." I got off the stage, looking around for anyone suspicious. The theater was filled with suspicious-looking people.

OK, Number One," I called as I sat in an open seat in the first row a few seats away from a decidedly overweight Lorre.

For the next hour they trouped up the stairs and became a blur. There were Lorres who looked fine but didn't sound anything like the real thing. There were Lorres who sounded fine but didn't look like the real thing. Then I had to remember that I wasn't looking for a Lorre look-alike, but a Lowry look-alike.

The line of actors and would-be actors went on doing Mr. Moto, the killer in *M* in fake and real German and, God help me, doing Joel Cairo in *The Maltese Falcon*.

"You will kindly put your hands behind your head and turn around," they said one after the other. "I am going to search you."

They emphasized different words, dragged out the sentence, rolled their eyes, and followed up with wild-eyed shouting of, "Where are the plans?"

Three Lorres sang songs. One of them, a woman who obviously specialized in Marlene Dietrich, sang "Falling in Love Again" in English and German with her eyes wide open.

I wrote down the numbers of those I didn't think were awful and asked all of them to leave their names and addresses with Wayne on the way out. When the theater was clear, Lorre and Jeremy came out on the stage.

"A very sobering experience," said Lorre, looking at the empty stage and puffing on a cigarette. "I may never be able to watch myself again."

"No Steinholtz?" I asked. "No one you recognized?"

"No," said Lorre.

"Well, that's one morning wasted," I said. "We didn't even find an actor for the Steistel Brothers."

"Steistel?" said Lorre. "That name I know from somewhere too."

"They made films back in Germany," I said. "Claim to be expressionists. Like loud trumpet solos."

"Oh, yes," smiled Lorre. "Quite eccentric. And they now have a studio here?"

"Miracle Pictures," I said.

"Mr. Lorre has a solution to your problem, Toby," Jeremy said, his eyes scanning the auditorium, his body close to Lorre's.

"To what?" I asked. "I feel like Warner Baxter in *42nd Street*. Someone shot the star and the crew is waiting for me to come up with Ruby Keeler."

"Why not," said Lorre, "suggest to the Steistels that they use the actor who looks most like your dead man . . ."

"Number Sixteen," I said, "but his voice . . ."

". . . and the voice of the one who sounds most like your dead man or like me," Lorre concluded.

"Number . . ." I began.

"Thirty-seven," said Lorre.

"Great idea," I said, "but that doesn't catch a killer. And Steinholtz seems to know you can identify him. But it beats hell out of me why he would want to keep from . . ."

"No," screamed a voice from the balcony behind us. Lorre, Jeremy, and I turned toward the sound and the turn was just enough to save Peter Lorre's life.

The shot came from the darkness of the balcony. It rocketed past Lorre and sent the drapery back as if it had been blown on by a hippo. I dropped to the floor and rolled off the stage and under the chairs in the first row as another shot came, and I watched Jeremy grab Lorre and roll backward off the stage.

"You all right, Jeremy?" I yelled.

"All right," called Jeremy calmly. "Both of us are fine."

The shooter shuffled in the balcony and I heard a door above me open. I sat up, didn't get shot at, and went for the fire exit on my left. I didn't have a gun but I was close to something and I didn't want to lose it. I went through the exit, found myself in an alley, and ran around to the front of the theater and into a crowd of Lorres who grabbed at me, asked questions, pleaded, and kept me from getting to the front entrance. Over their heads I saw a figure in a black raincoat dash out through the door of the Hitching Post. The figure's collar was pulled up to hide his face. Under his arm was a flower box that could have held all kinds of weapons.

"We'll call the winner tomorrow," I said. "Now if you'll just let me . . ."

The guy in the raincoat moved to a dark Chevy waiting near the curb as I struggled to get free. The driver of the Chevy pulled into traffic on Hollywood, squealed rubber in first gear and shot around onto Vine. I pulled a pair of hands from my sleeve, did a jump left worthy of the Galloping Ghost, and dashed around the corner of my car. I could see the Chevy half a block away, and knew that I could either catch it or attract enough attention to stop him. I could do that if I could drive my car, which I couldn't. My left rear tire had been slashed.

I went back into the theater and told Jeremy to stay close to Lorre for the next two hours, to go back to his office at the Farraday. Lorre was quiet. I expected him to be shaken, but the look on his face wasn't fear. It was closer to anger. I didn't push or pursue it. I found Wayne and promised him an extra five bucks for helping. He said he'd send Lorre the bill for the bullet holes in the screen. There wouldn't be a charge for the curtain since the bullet holes couldn't be seen.

I went back out on Vine where Gunther Wherthman stood leaning on his cane.

"You saved Peter Lorre's life," I told him as I opened the trunk of my Crosley.

"I could think of nothing else to do but shout," Gunther said softly. "I did not think I had the ability to overcome the shooter."

"You did fine," I said.

"And you were correct about the killer," said Gunther as people walked past us. "Would you like some assistance in changing your tire?"

"No, thanks, I'm used to dirty work," I said.

"Then, if you have no further need for my help, I shall return to my work," Gunther said.

"Gunther, I'm going to get Shelly out of there. If I don't call you in two hours, call Jeremy at the Farraday and tell him where I am. Then you two can come in and rescue us."

"I think it would be much more reasonable to inform the police immediately," he said, as I jacked up the car.

"Much more reasonable," I agreed.

"But you do not plan to do so."

"I do not plan to do so," I confirmed, turning the tire iron.

There was nothing more to say. Gunther took off and I changed my tire and dropped the flat one off at No-neck Arnie's to be fixed. Then I headed off to rescue Shelly.

13

"What'll it be?" said Connie, the drooping owner of Connie's on Beverly.

"Coffee, a sinker, and some information," I said, sitting down at the counter.

Connie pushed herself away from the wall, put down her newspaper, and dropped her cigarette in an ashtray on the counter.

"Coffee coming up," she said, moving to the tarnished pot on the burner in front of me. "Pick your own sinker."

A pile of semistale doughnuts and something that looked as if it might once have been a pecan roll sat in a plate near my elbow. I picked the least deadly looking doughnut and put it on the edge of the saucer Connie placed in front of me with a cup of coffee.

"What information you need?" she asked, coughing.

"Eskian's," I said, breaking the doughnut in half and dunking it in the brown, steamy liquid. "How long he had his hardware store?"

"Maybe eight years, something like that," she said, folding her bony arms.

"You know his kid?"

"Robert? Sure," she said. "Odd kid."

"What's he look like?" I asked, munching on the last piece of soggy doughnut and reaching for another.

She described him and I nodded.

"One more question," I said. "Is there another way into Eskian's besides the front door?"

Connie laughed and the laugh turned into a smoker's hacking cough. I thought she might die on the counter. I reached over and patted her on the back. She recovered slowly.

"You look too much like a crook to be one," she said, standing back.

"Not sure I buy your logic, Connie, but I'm not a crook. I've got a feeling a friend is somewhere in Eskian's and he doesn't want to be there."

"Never much liked Eskian or his kid," she said. "Something creepy about them both, you know?"

"I know," I said, standing up and pulling change out of my pocket. "What's the damage?"

"Make it a dime," she said. I dropped a quarter on the counter.

She picked it up and put her tongue in her cheek thinking and said, "What the hell. Go through my kitchen, out the back door. You'll see a fence. Other side of the fence is a little space, all concrete. You'll see a couple of windows. That's the back of Eskian's."

"I owe you one, Connie," I said, moving to the end of the counter.

"Hey," she said, retrieving her cigarette and newspaper, "if I had all the ones guys like you owe me, I'd be living on the beach."

I went through Connie's kitchen, which was small, clean, and smelled like grilled onions. The wooden fence outside her rear door was chest-high and wobbly, but I climbed it without much trouble and dropped on the other side onto a small, cement-covered yard. Two full garbage cans stood near the fence. The windows were right where Connie said they would be. I tried the window on the right. The latch was rusty and would have snapped with a good pull, but I didn't want any noise if I could help it. I moved to the other window. It was latched too, but the latch was just barely in place. I pushed the window up a touch with my fingertips and created a narrow gap pressing against the lock. I found a long, rusty bolt in one of the garbage cans and wedged it under the window. Using the bolt as a lever, I sweated the window up until it squealed past the latch.

Now there was enough room under the window for my fingers. I lifted the window and looked inside. It was a windowless single-door storage room filled with barrels and sacks. I climbed through the window, pushed the latch out of the way, closed the window, and latched it before I turned into the room toward the door.

I took my shoes off and padded across the room. The door opened without much noise. So far, so good. I was in a large basement room that smelled like leaking gasoline. There was one small window letting in enough light for me to make out the broad shadows of the room and to see a door about ten feet in front of me with light coming under it. I looked around for a weapon and found a barrel full of shovels. I pulled out one of the shovels as quietly as I could, put my shoes back on, and went for the door with the light under it.

With the shovel in my left hand, I reached out with my right and opened the door slowly. There were no sounds inside the room. I stuck my head through and saw Sheldon Minck in the center of the room, tied in a chair. He was wearing a day-old beard and his dirty white smock. A single forty-watt bulb dangled on a frayed cord over his head.

"Shel," I whispered, hoisting the shovel in both hands like Stan Hack ready for a high inside pitch.

Shelly looked up, twitched his nose, and squinted in my general direction.

"Toby?" he shouted.

"Shel, be quiet," I said stepping into the room.

The room held four wooden chairs, including the one Shelly was tied onto. In the corner to the right was a wooden stairway going up to a door that must lead to Eskian's hardware store.

"Toby," he yelled. "These are crazy people here. Sadists. They feed me candy and water and they don't let me brush my teeth."

"I'll get you out, Shel, but be quiet," I said, watching the door at the top of the stairs and moving in front of Shelly.

"I can't see," he said. "My glasses. They have my glasses."

"You need a bath, Shel," I said, fishing in my pocket for the glasses.

"I need a cigar," he said. "My glasses."

I put the glasses on his nose, watched him open his eyes wide, and whispered, "I'll get these ropes off and we're out of here. Just be quiet, for God's sake."

"Too late," Shelly cried, looking over my shoulder.

Before I could turn, something clanged off my skull. Shelly later confirmed that it was the shovel I had put down. It was probably a good thing that I was slow in turning. If I'd moved quicker, I'd probably have lost the rest of my nose. Instead, I merely lost consciousness.

Koko the Clown danced in front of me and shook his finger to let me know I had made another mistake. I waited for Koko to lead me out of the hole with no sides I was floating in, but he just kept shaking his head. Finally, I just gave up, closed my eyes, and let Koko dance on the back of my brain.

Somewhere in that darkness Mickey Mouse asked me if I was all right. I tried to tell Mickey that I could use a little help, but the words wouldn't come out and he just kept asking. I opened my eyes and Bobby Parotti stood in front of me, shovel in hand, asking, no longer in a Mickey Mouse voice. "Are you all right?"

I tried to move my hands. They were tied behind my back to the chair was I seated in. I tried to move my legs. They were tied.

"Are you all right?" he repeated.

"No, I'm not all right," I groaned. "You hit me in the head with a shovel. You could have killed me."

"I'm sorry," he said, putting down the shovel.

"This is saving me?" asked Shelly on my right.

I glanced at him. He was furiously trying to work his glasses back up his nose so he could see.

"I had to," said Bobby. "I want you to understand. You were really nice in the zoo. You helped me. I didn't . . ."

"Your father," I said. "Where is he?"

Bobby looked at the stairway with fear and then back at me.

"He'll kill you if he finds you here," Bobby whispered.

"Then don't let him find us here," I whispered back. "Let us go. You didn't kill anybody, did you?"

"No," he said.

"If he comes and kills us, you'll be a killer," I said.

"Yes," agreed Shelly. "You'd be a killer."

"Don't say any more," he said "I've got to think."

"Think," I said.

"But think fast," Shelly cried, looking at the door at the top of the stairs.

"He'll kill us, Bobby. You know he'll kill us," I said. "You want to see us all over the floor? He'll make you clean it up."

"No more. I don't want to hear any more," Bobby shouted and ran out of the room through the same door I'd come in. The door slammed shut behind him.

"Quick, Shel," I whispered, pain throbbing in my head, "tip your chair over and slide over here next to me. I think you can get your mouth high enough to bite these ropes. But hurry."

"Bite the ropes?" Shelly groaned. "You know what that would do to my teeth? I'm a dentist. What kind of example would it be for my patients for God's sake if I went around chewing on dirty ropes?"

"Shelly," I said through clenched teeth, "they could come back and kill us."

"Let me think about it," Shelly said.

"How long was I out?"

"Who knows? A while. An hour, maybe more. Time passes so fast when you're having fun."

"You've got no time to think," I said. "Shit."

I tipped my chair over and it clattered against the cement. My cheek hit the floor and I almost went out again but I looked over at the doors. No one came running in. I crawled slowly in agony toward Shelly and worked my way behind him. My mouth was just high enough to reach the rope on his wrists.

"I'll fix your teeth for nothing, Toby. Honest to God," Shelly said. "I swear it. Free X rays."

"I'll settle for your thanks," I said. "And a complete cleaning of the office the way you promised."

I dug my teeth into the rope.

"I just cleaned the place," wailed Shelly.

"A month ago," I said, spitting out hemp. I bit furiously for about a minute and said, "Pull, Shel. I think you can break . . ."

And Sheldon gave a pull that tore the last strands just as the door at the top of the stairs clattered open.

"Do something," Shelly screamed.

"You're the one with his hands free," I reminded him. "I'm tied up on the floor with a broken skull."

"What the heck is going, going on down here?" Paul Eskian said angrily, hurrying down the stairs with a rifle in his hands. "You," he said pointing at Shelly. "Just you sit, sit, sit there."

"I'm sitting," Sheldon cried, and put his hands on his lap.

Eskian moved over to me and pulled me up.

"Bobby," he called.

Bobby came running back into the room and picked up the shovel, ready to bash me again.

"Bobby," Eskian said, "why didn't you come and get, get me when he woke up like I told, told, told you to?"

"You're not going to kill them," Bobby said.

"No," Eskian said sarcastically. "I'm going to untie them and let them go so they, they, they can tell the police and I can be hanged. Bobby, if we kill, kill them I'm safe. You're safe."

"What are you people talking about?" Shelly squealed.

"It's simple, Shel," I said. "Paul Eskian here has a hardware store upstairs. His real name is Steinholtz. He's a former Nazi. That's his son, Robert, who uses the name Bobby Parotti because he wants to be in movies. He probably made up the name."

"It's my mother's name," Bobby said.

"Peters . . ." Eskian began.

"Let me finish explaining to Shelly," I said, stalling in the hope that Jeremy would be momentarily bursting through the door. "He should at least know why he's dying. You can give me a hand by filling in when I miss something."

"Talk," said Eskian.

"OK," I said. "Bobby works for a company called Miracle Pictures. He thought he could make a few bucks for his dad by getting the guys who run the company to shoot a scene on the roof. But a coincidence happened. The star of this cheap little movie was Mildred's friend, Klausfueler or Kindem or Lowry."

"Too damn many names," Shelly said.

Not enough names, I thought, and went on with my tale. "Klausfueler recognized our friend Eskian as Steinholtz. He had known him back in Vienna. The real Peter Lorre knew him, too. Lorre's real name, by the way, is Ladislav Lowenstein. Was it blackmail?"

"Blackmail," agreed Eskian. "He was going to, to blackmail me."

"So," I went on, "I pulled up in front of the hardware store the other morning and Eskian here saw me. I asked too many questions and he thought I might be in it with Klausfueler. How am I doing?"

"Very, very, very well," said Eskian. I didn't know if he was stammering or complimenting me.

"He went through my car. Not hard with his collection of keys. Found my gun, came up the stairs, shot Klausfueler, and threw the gun down. Later, when I came around asking questions, he made up a man with a black coat."

"I don't care about all this, Toby," Sheldon moaned.

"You'll love it, Sheldon," I snapped. "Our friend Steinholtz here went to Klausfueler's room at the Ravenswood Hotel and found a photograph of himself, Klausfueler, and the real Peter Lorre. So, he decided to go after the real Lorre too, but he did something he thought was really clever. After he shot Klausfueler he picked a random Peter Lorre imitator and killed him. Then he took a shot at another one and tried to run another one down. You want to know why?"

"No," wept Shelly. "I don't know what the hell you're talking about."

"I'll tell you why. To draw the investigation away from the murder on the roof, to make it look like some lunatic was going after Peter Lorres, and that it might be someone other than the people on the roof. Paul Eskian and his son Bobby were just innocent, confused bystanders. But I kept concentrating on the murder up on the roof. The cops were running all over the city but not me. So . . ."

"I had to stop, stop, stop you," Eskian said.

"Another mistake," I said. "When I didn't get scared away by bullets, dead pigeons, and bloody messages you decided to kidnap Shelly and threaten me on the phone, but you couldn't call me on the phone, even with a disguised voice. Your stammer would give you away. That's why you had Bobby make the calls, but Bobby didn't do so well."

"Are you done?" Eskian said.

"Not even close," I said, trying not to look at the door at the top of the stairs, which was slowly opening.

"That's all I have time, time for," said Eskian, stepping toward me and leveling the rifle at my head.

"No," said Bobby.

"No," said Shelly.

"Steinholtz," came Peter Lorre's voice from the dark at the top of the stairs. It was a command. Steinholtz paused, rifle still aimed at my face, and looked toward the stairs.

"Oh God," cried Bobby as Peter Lorre calmly walked down the stairs, pausing near the bottom to light a cigarette.

"I never expected to see you again," Lorre said, stepping forward into the circle of yellow light from the dangling bulb above our heads. "I thought you would be a brownshirt colonel by now."

Steinholtz said something in German. In German he didn't stammer.

Lorre answered in German but his answer was clipped, angry.

"So you just make, make, make it easier for me," Steinholtz said his finger closing on the trigger. "I shoot all, all, all three of you and I'm safe."

"You are a fool," spat Lorre in his best Peter Lorre imitation. "Do you think I would come here alone after you tried to shoot me? Do you think I would tell no one? Look."

He pointed up the stairs where the hulking form of Jeremy Butler filled the doorway.

"You are pathetic," Lorre said with a sneer and a disgusted shake of his head.

"They were after me," Steinholtz said, sweat forming on his brow and upper lip. "The Nazis were after me. I had, had, had, had to leave, had to hide from them. I lied about my background when I came here but I lied to hide from the Nazis who might come after me. Then Klausfueler threatened to tell the FBI that I was a Nazi. It was ironic."

Steinholtz's hand quivered slightly as he let out a laugh, but the barrel of the rifle was still aimed somewhere in the general direction of my face.

"I don't see anything funny about this," moaned Shelly.

"This excuse for a man is not laughing," Lorre said with disdain, stepping within a few feet of Steinholtz. "That is panic, hysterical panic. This is not worthy of you."

"Dad," wept Bobby in the corner.

"No," shouted Steinholtz. "I'll kill you all. I'll, I'll, I'll find a . . ."

But before he could tell us what he would find a way to do, Peter Lorre stepped forward and slapped the big man, slapped him with a loud thwack.

"We're dead," Shelly said under his breath. "Dead."

But we weren't dead. Steinholtz stepped back and let the rifle sag at his side.

"You kill people," Lorre shouted, his voice a mad threat. "You killed my cousin. You killed innocent people. You'd try to kill me? You'd try to kill my friends? You're still a Nazi."

Even though Steinholtz had the rifle he backed away looking for help, but not even his son was prepared to stand up to the angry, shouting little man with the huge eyes and the hair falling over his forehead. Lorre stepped forward and slapped Steinholtz again. The bigger man yelped once and raced toward the stairs. Jeremy stepped down and Steinholtz thought better of that exit. He shoved his way past Lorre, who grabbed for him, and knocked down his son Bobby as he went out the door I had come through.

"Jeremy," I yelled. "Get him. There's a window through there and a way out."

Jeremy leapt down the stairs and raced toward the door Steinholtz had dashed through. I'm sure he would have caught him if Bobby hadn't roused himself with tears in his eyes, picked up the shovel, and swung with both hands at Jeremy who was running full steam toward the open door. The blow probably would have killed him if it had gotten him in the head, but the ex-wrestler threw his hand up and caught the steel blade across his palm. The metal cut into his palm and Jeremy rolled toward Bobby and into him, sending the kid flying across the basement. The shovel shot into the air and Jeremy caught it in his bleeding hand.

I've never seen Jeremy angry, but as he stood holding that shovel in his bloody hand, standing over the cowering Bobby who crawled backwards, whimpering into a corner, something dark crossed that broad face.

"The paternal knot," Lorre said softly to Jeremy, who held the shovel in one hand over his head. "The mythological archetype. The son flees the father, hates the father, but cannot escape the tie, the loyalty. Isn't it Keats who . . ."

"Byron," said Jeremy evenly. "It was Byron who got to the heart of the conflict. Keats only lyricized."

"Of course," said Lorre, shaking his head. "Byron."

Jeremy looked at the shovel, bent his knee, and calmly broke the thick shaft in two over his knee. Bobby shrank back into the corner as Jeremy moved forward and lifted him by the arm with his undamaged hand.

"No one is going to hurt you," he said gently. "I'll heal much faster than you will."

While Jeremy held the weeping Bobby, Peter Lorre untied me and Shelly. When he finished, I got up on unsteady legs, touched my swollen head, and looked at him. Lorre was even shakier than I was. He pulled out a cigarette but his hands were too shaky to light it. I took the match and did it for him.

"Hell of a performance," I said.

"You think so?" he answered softly. "I've never been terribly good at improvisation. I relied a bit too heavily on my memory of Raskolnikov in *Crime and Punishment*. I mean the later scenes when he is being—"

"I don't care," Shelly interrupted, slouching toward the stairs. "I really don't care about your performance, about any of this, not any of this. I'm a dentist. I shouldn't have to worry about people."

"Let's get Bobby to the police," I said to Jeremy, "and let's get your hand taken care of."

"Pity there was no camera," Lorre sighed.

14

That should have been the end of it. At the hospital after we turned Bobby over to the police and told Steve Seidman our story, Lorre gave me a check for $150 to cover three days' work and a bonus. He refused to wait for an itemized bill. I pointed out to him that Steinholtz was still out there somewhere, but he reasonably argued that Steinholtz no longer had a reason to kill him. Steinholtz's identity was no longer secret. Lorre thanked me for the adventure and insisted on taking a cab home.

Jeremy's hand took twenty stitches—twelve less, he pointed out, than it took to sew him back together after Mad Dog Morey bit him in the leg in their match at the L.A. Olympics in '34. A doctor I didn't know looked at my dented skull and recommended hospitalization and tests. Then an orderly brought my hospital medical record and the M.D. decided that I was a hopeless case whose record clearly demonstrated that I should have had enough head injuries from previous attacks to earn me full-time membership in a home for the permanently brain-damaged.

"Have you ever considered another line of work?" the doc asked. He was still young enough to hope that words might make a difference.

"Professional hockey," I said, "but I'd have to learn to skate and move to Canada."

Shelly had nothing to say. He wanted to go home to his wife. From the hospital lobby he called Mildred, who said she was pleased that he wasn't dead, but that he could not come home and that her brother Michael would be dropping off all of his clothes at the office.

I drove Shelly back to the Farraday. Jeremy took a cab. We both knew from experience that he wouldn't fit into my Crosley. When I pulled up in front of the Farraday, I told Shelly he could bunk with me for a few days if he wanted to, but that I had filched his Buddha from the house when Mildred wasn't looking and had put it in the car trunk. He'd probably have enough for a hotel if he wanted to be alone.

"I'm going to a hotel," Shelly said. "I've got plenty in the Buddha."

"Lorre just paid me a hundred and fifty, Shel," I said to the forlorn dentist, who stood on Hoover Street in his dirty white smock looking lost and betrayed.

"That's all right," he said, "I've got about nineteen thousand dollars in the Buddha?"

"Nineteen thousand?" I said.

"Gold filings, a few investments," said Shelly, looking at the Farraday entrance.

"Mildred will be after it," I warned.

"She doesn't know about it," he said. I got the Buddha out of the trunk, handed it to him, and watched him go through the Farraday entrance.

I stopped at a small grocery on the way home and picked up a few things. It was around six when I got back to Mrs. Plaut's and ran up the stairs, determined to hit my mattress clothes and all and not wake up for a week until my head stopped hurting. I made it to the top of the stairs, setting a new record, when Mrs. Plaut's voice shrilled up at me.

"Mr. Peelers," she cried.

"I'm in pain," I said, continuing toward my door.

"You had a call," she shouted.

"Tell me about it later," I said, reaching my door.

"The stuttering man said it was important," she said, "but it is no skin off my knuckles."

I stopped and went to the railing to look down at her.

"The stuttering man?" I said. "What was his message?"

She paused, looked up at me with exasperation, and fished a crumpled sheet from her apron pocket.

"Come to I. Magnin's on Wilshire alone as soon as is possible, mens' furnishings, and I will turn myself in."

"That's all?" I asked.

"Verbatim," she said.

"Thanks," I said and moved to my room where I turned on the light and walked slowly to my refrigerator. I prepared myself a glass of milk and a bowl of shredded wheat topped with a banana.

"I'm too old for this," I said, gritting my teeth against the pain in my head and shoveling in banana slices and soggy wheat.

I could have called my brother, or Steve Seidman, or the fire department, or the FBI, and gone to bed, but I knew I wouldn't. I finished my dinner, piled the dishes in the sink, changed my shirt, turned off the light, closed the door, and moved on unwilling legs down the stairs, stopping to knock at Mrs. Plaut's door.

"Yes, Mr. Peelers?" she said primly.

"Your husband had a gun," I said. "You showed it to me once."

"The hog leg," she said. "Six-shooter, gift from Wyatt Earp when Earp bought some land from the mister in Fresno."

"You told me it's still in working order," I said.

"Oiled and ready to ward off lecherous attacks at night," she confirmed.

"Could I borrow it for a few hours?" I said.

She adjusted her hearing aid and looked at me as if I were mentally retarded.

"It is," she said very slowly, "an heirloom."

"I want to show it to a friend, a friend who appreciates fine firearms," I lied. "He's the one who called. He's only in for a few hours from Sante Fe. I mentioned your husband's weapon and he begged me to let him see it. It would mean a lot to him. His mother is not well."

"I fail to see how the illness of his mother relates to this," she said, "but seeing as how you will be helping with the rubber drive and the grease collection, I'll allow you several hours, but it must be back in my hands by bedtime or I shall be filled with fury."

She fetched the oversized weapon and placed it in my hands. I took it carefully, thanked her, tried to find a way to hide it under my coat and gave up. Night had fallen when I stepped out on the street and headed for my car. I opened the small trunk and pulled out a crumpled shopping bag. I dropped the mister's hog leg in, got in the driver's seat, and headed for Wilshire.

I didn't turn on the radio. I knew what the sound would to do my head. I just drove until I pulled past Magnin's in time to see Rudy Vallee give a last wave and a "Hi-ho everybody, from the Victory Window."

By the time I had parked the car a few blocks away and walked back, Rudy Vallee was no longer in the window and people were streaming out of the store. I tucked my shopping bag under my arm and elbowed my way past a pair of heavyweight sisters.

"Sorry," the watchman at the door said, "closing time."

"I've got an exchange to make, urgent," I said.

"Tomorrow," he said.

He was big, dark and not looking forward to a long night. The plate on his uniformed chest said his name was Arlen Murchison. The look on his face said Arlen Murchison was in no mood for charity.

"It'll just take a minute," I said.

"Tomorrow," Murchison repeated, pushing me out of the way to let a straggler out.

"Tomorrow will be too late," I said.

Murchison shrugged and looked into the store, which seemed to be clear. Lights were going out inside. There was no one on the sidewalk now except me and a few people scurrying for the bus and their cars.

"There's a killer in there," I said.

Murchison looked at me with some interest and decided I was a loony.

"Wrong," he said. "There are two killers in there, both German shepherds and they don't like people prowling I. Magnin's after closing. Now you just back off, sober up or see your doctor, and come back tomorrow. Or, better yet, don't come back tomorrow."

He started to close the door on me and I reached into my shopping bag and pulled out the six-shooter.

"I'm coming in," I said.

"I had to get a goddamn loony," he sighed, backing up. "Come back from vacation and the first night, the first minute I get a loony. OK. Come in. You'll get your neck ripped open but come in."

I stepped in, keeping the big gun low and blocking it from the street with my body.

"Keep your hands down," I said, "and let's walk to menswear."

"You gonna steal a pair of socks?" Murchison asked. He had seen it all.

"I'm going to catch a killer. You and I are going to catch a killer," I said. "You're going to be a hero."

He led me through the darkened store past staring dummies and glass counters that caught our passing images.

"My bet is that he's hiding someplace, waiting," I said. "He may have given up, but my bet is that he wants me. And he thinks it's ironic that he should get me in the same department where Lowry or Kindem or Klausfueler worked. He likes irony."

"Mac," Murchison said, "you are out of your mind."

"He wants me, Murchison," I said, glancing around into the darkness as we walked.

"He wants you?" Murchison repeated, walking ahead and

shaking his head, unwilling to humor the lunatic behind him. "There are two German shepherds that are going to want you if you don't put that thing away. I'm willing to let you out and give you five minutes before I call the police."

"Keep walking," I said, "And get down. He could be any—"

The shot came straight down the aisle toward us. We both saw the flash of the gun, heard the crack. Murchison went down as if someone had kicked his right leg out from behind.

"Son of a bitch," he yelled.

"I told you," I said, gripping the hog leg in two hands and pulling the trigger. The gun jolted me backward and the bullet screamed down the aisle in the direction the shot had come from. There wasn't much chance that I had hit him or come even close, but at least I had let Steinholtz know that I had a gun.

"I mean to kill, kill, kill you, Peters," he said from the darkness. "I've got nothing, no son, no business, no life, nothing because of you."

"Because of me?" I shouted. "You better go over the story again. You wrote it, not me."

Murchison held his knee and rolled groaning in the aisle.

Steinholtz took another shot, hit a glass counter that shattered about ten feet behind me, and stood up to get a better shot. I had Mr. Plaut's six-shooter resting on a tie display rack and a reasonably good bead on his big frame against an exit light but I didn't get to shoot. Something growled behind me. Two somethings growled behind me and Murchison moaned, "Heidi, Trudi, no."

But Heidi and Trudi had minds of their own and came scuttering toward me. I got up and Steinholtz took another shot that thudded into a post near my head as I dropped the hog leg and ran toward the front of the store with the Nazi dogs at my heels.

I got to the Victory Window, jumped in, and closed the door behind me—which is where I started this tale.

*   *   *

Two minutes later, with the door coming down, I was ready to call it a lifetime when I heard a shot. The dogs threw themselves once more onto what was left of the door and another shot cracked through the door and shattered the Victory Window, sending a spray of glass across the sidewalk and onto Wilshire, hitting a passing Olds that lost control and skidded over the curb.

I let go of the door and jumped out of the window onto the sidewalk. The dogs came bursting through the door, looked at me on the street with longing, and stopped.

I stood, staring back at them, waiting for them to come at me, waiting to be ripped to pieces in front of I. Magnin's where I'd be swept up with the glass in the morning. A man got out of the car that had skidded over the curb. He gave me a dirty look. He was about to give me more, but he saw the dogs in the broken window and jumped back in his Olds.

My legs were about to give out but I stood staring at the dogs till Murchison stumbled into the Victory Window, a trail of blood trickling down the leg of his uniform, a whistle in his mouth.

He blew the whistle but no sound came out. The dogs turned and ran back into the store.

"He's dead," Murchison called. "I shot the son of a bitch. Will you get your ass back in here, call me an ambulance, and tell me what the hell is going on."

The hospital wasn't glad to see me again. Steve Seidman wasn't glad to see me either, but he didn't call my brother. We agreed to give Murchison full credit for catching Steinholtz and leave my name out of it. This was fine with Murchison on condition that he never see me again.

By midnight I was back at Mrs. Plaut's. The lights were out. I knocked at her door and waited till she came in her night dress, opened the door, looked at me, and accepted the six-shooter.

"Did he appreciate the weapon?" she said.

"Enormously," I said and she closed the door. I started up the stairs more slowly than I had ever taken them before and Mrs. Plaut's door opened behind me.

"I almost forgot," she said. "There was a telephone message for you. I left it on your door."

With that, she closed her door again and I finished making my way up the stairs and across the hall.

I tore the piece of paper off the tack on my door, went into my room, turned on the light, and tried to focus on Mrs. Plaut's printed message. There was a number and the words, "Call Major Castle on General MacArthur's staff at this number."

I switched off the light, took off my shoes, and fell onto my mattress without undressing. Major Castle and General MacArthur would have to wait till morning.